The Wolf of Harrow Hall

CHRISTINE POPE

DARK VALENTINE PRESS

THE WOLF OF HARROW HALL

ISBN: 978-0692662311
Copyright © 2016 by Christine Pope
Published by Dark Valentine Press

Cover design by Ravven
Book layout by Indie Author Services

To learn more about this author, go to
www.christinepope.com.

The Wolf of Harrow Hall

Chapter One

I stared down at the meager collection of silver coins as they lay on the worn surface of the kitchen table, then looked up at my grandmother in dismay. "This is all we have left? But where has the rest of it gone?"

She pushed a strand of greying hair away from her face. Sometime during her last fabric dyeing session, that lock must have come loose from the neat coil—still heavy and thick—at the back of her head. "'Where has the rest of it gone'?" she repeated. My grandmother was not the sort to let the various blows the world had visited upon her weaken her spirit, but in that moment, I thought I could hear a weariness in her voice she couldn't completely conceal. "Why, to patch the roof, and to purchase a new goat after the wolves got Sissi, and to pay Garrit for another load of firewood after the last storm, and—"

"I see," I cut in. Perhaps that was rude of me, but in that moment, I did not wish to hear the tally of our troubles once again. Truly, this past autumn and the beginning of the winter that followed had not been kind to us. And now, with the turn of the year rapidly approaching, so, too, approached the time when we must pay our tithe to the Mark of North Eredor, so that we might live yet another year here in the cottage where I had been born.

I had never seen the lord of our land, for his capital of Tarenmar lay several days' ride to the south. Indeed, in all my twenty-one years, I had never seen much of anything beyond the forest of Sarisfell, which covered many leagues to either side of the village where I had been born. No doubt the Mark and his court would have thought our little hamlet of Kerolton small and mean, but it—and the people who lived there—were all I knew.

My thoughts churned as I considered what our next course of action should be. Our household was small, and consisted of only my grandmother and myself, for my grandfather had died of a fever some five years earlier, when I had barely passed into my sixteenth year. He had been an accomplished woodsman, and had hunted and trapped in the woods of Sarisfell, providing the merchants in Tarenmar with beautiful furs to adorn the ladies at court. Our worry over the loss of the income my grandfather had brought in was only exceeded by our grief at his passing, for he had been a cheerful sort, never one to allow a harsh winter or a meager meal to subdue his sunny nature.

In those five years since his passing, my grandmother and I had worked doubly hard at spinning and dyeing, transforming the wool from our neighbors' sheep into sturdy fabrics. But often those same neighbors wished to trade their wool for the cloth we finished for them, or to barter for other necessities, and so we never had much in the way of ready coin, barely enough to purchase those items we could procure no other way, and to scrape together the ready for our taxes.

To most, those taxes would not seem so terribly onerous, for the Mark was not a greedy man and did not expect more of his subjects than they could comfortably give. Now, though, even that modest sum seemed to me more than a king's ransom.

"Well," I said, doing my best not to sigh, "I think I must go speak to Amery and see if he can find it in himself to loan us the necessary sum. His flock is thriving, and he is certainly not suffering for ready cash."

Amery Willar was the richest man in our village. More to the point, he had once wished to marry my mother and give me his name. My mother had declined his suit, and had disappeared from our lives not long afterward, but Amery had never seemed to hold her betrayal against me. Instead, he always treated me with a rough kindness somewhat tinged with regret, as if he still wished that I might have been his daughter, even though he had been happily married these seventeen years or so.

At any rate, I thought he was the most likely person to approach about borrowing the required sum. There was one other in the village who was nearly as prosperous as Amery, but I doubted he would look kindly upon me asking him for a loan.

My grandmother appeared even more troubled after I made my suggestion. "I am not sure that is the best thing to try, Bettany."

"What else would you have me do?" I shot back. "I know you are too proud to ask anyone for money. I am not sure how well that pride would serve you in a debtor's gaol, but I would rather not find out."

She was silent then, her gaze not meeting mine. I looked at the heavy grey streaks in her dark hair and wondered when they had first appeared. The year Grandfather died? Truly, I could not seem to remember. She'd been beautiful and young-seeming for her age, and then appeared to age decades almost overnight. Not that I could blame her.

Our existence had not been easy for me, either, although it had yet to cause any grey strands to appear in my hair, and my face bore no real signs of the heavy work that kept us occupied from the time the sun rose—and sometimes before—until it sank into the west each night. But I knew that time would eventually catch up to me, just as it had to her.

Unfortunately, there didn't seem to be terribly much I could do about it.

Taking my grandmother's silence as tacit agreement with my plan, or at least as a disinclination to argue further, I went to the peg next to the door where my cloak hung and swung it around my shoulders. The weather had been brooding and grey, yet no storms had yet come, even though the clouds felt thick with snow.

Our cottage lay somewhat outside the boundaries of Kerolton, for my grandfather had always averred that it was better to be close to the animals in order to trap them. On fine sunny days, I did not mind the walk. Now, though, the ice in the chill air seemed to penetrate even the thick wool of my cloak and through to my plain bodice and skirt of wool and linen beneath.

No doubt the cloak I wore was an incongruous note in those somber winter woods, with their dark, snow-dusted firs and pines and the bare, slender branches of the birch and elm trees. The wool had dyed unevenly, so it was bright scarlet in patches and deeper crimson in others. We could not sell the fabric, and so my grandmother, who was a better seamstress than I, had fashioned it into a new cloak, as my old one had become quite threadbare. The red cloak was warm enough, true, but I thought it was far too conspicuous. I had already learned the harsh lesson that it was better not to attract too much attention.

Even on that bitterly cold morning, birds still sang from the barren branches overhead, and I heard rustlings in the dead undergrowth that could have been squirrels, or perhaps a fox. They had grown more adventurous over the past few years, now that my grandfather was not around to trap them.

Kerolton came into view after a brisk walk of a quarter-hour or so. Smoke streamed upward from numerous chimneys, a paler grey against the lowering sky. On a fine day, I would have seen people going to the well to draw water, or driving their sheep down the narrow lanes of the hamlet, or perhaps loitering around the doorway of Hamm's tavern, but not today. Now, all the doors were latched, and heavy shutters had been closed over the windows as a barrier against the cold.

I heard rather than saw the light plodding of many hooves against the hard-packed snowy ground, and turned to see Amery Willar approaching, his felt hat pulled down low over his eyes and a scarf knitted in a bewildering array of colors knotted tightly around his throat. Despite his muffled state, I could still see surprise flicker over his features as he caught sight of me.

"Bettany Sendris!" he exclaimed, coming to a stop. His two great black and white shepherd dogs immediately ranged back toward the flock of sheep that had been following him, making sure they stopped as well and did not surround us. "What do you here, with this storm approaching?"

Storm? I flicked a skeptical eye skyward and shrugged. That snow had been threatening for the past two days and still showed no sign of falling. Perhaps it wouldn't reach Kerolton at all, but would only pass over the forest, as these things often did around the turn of the year. It was in Janver that we would see the truly dangerous storms sweep through North Eredor.

"I fear it is not on pleasant business," I said, hugging my gaudy cloak more closely about me. Yes, no snow had yet fallen, but still the air had a bite to it I did not like much. "There is no easy way for me to say this, Amery, and so I must beg your indulgence. This past season has not been kind to my grandmother and me, and it seems we are far short in the count of what we must send to the Mark as our tithe for the year. I was hoping—no, I am praying—that you might come to our aid. I swear that we will repay you when summer comes, and I am able to range the forest and gather the ingredients I need to compound my dyes."

A certain sadness entered his kind blue eyes. He was not a handsome man, but there was a pleasantness in his face that I had always admired. From the way he hesitated before answering, I knew his reply would not be one I wished to hear.

"I wish it were in my power to do so, Bettany, but I suppose you have heard that Vianna was betrothed this last Octevre?"

"Yes," I replied. I already knew what was coming next, but it would have been rude for me to interrupt. Instead, I waited with an already sinking heart as he continued.

"Well, I must give six head of sheep as her dowry, and she must have a gown of fine-woven wool from Tarenmar, and none of this homemade—" He broke off there and sent me an apologetic look. "That is not to say that what you and your grandmother produce is not good and sturdy, and worthy of many years of wear. But Vianna wishes for something more befitting the occasion."

"Of course," I said. Vianna had somehow turned out prettier than either of her parents' looks might have promised, and so had acquired the airs to go with her beauty. Her betrothed was a handsome young man, the son of the local ironmonger.

Amery stepped closer and laid a gloved hand on mine, which was encased in a knitted wool mitten. We could not afford the fine leather gloves that Amery wore. "Believe me, it is not easy for me to say this to you, Bettany. But I am no rich merchant from Tarenmar, and I do not have the wherewithal to help you and still give my daughter the wedding she wishes. You do understand."

"I understand," I said clearly. "I am no daughter of yours, and you must do your duty by your blood."

His forehead creased in a frown. "You know that I wish I could have looked on you as a daughter."

"I do. But my mother's whims prevented such a thing from coming to pass, and now I must think of some other way to keep us from the debtor's gaol."

That remark only caused his frown to deepen, and I saw his gaze flicker toward a house on the opposite side of the village square, a two-story edifice with real glass windows that had been brought in all the way from Tarenmar. "Perhaps you should reconsider your decision, Bettany."

"No," I said, my voice firm. "I think I would rather languish in prison than be Clem's wife."

"Surely you don't mean that."

Oh, but I do. Clem Wisegrot was the second-richest man in the village, one who had a royal grant to cut the trees in the forest and turn them into lumber, although he employed several men to do the actual wood cutting. At forty-two, he was also twice my age, with three children from his late wife, who no doubt died young to escape his company. I'd long held the opinion that Clem's proposal to me had everything to do with his desire to have a keeper for his unruly brood and very little to do with my own charms.

I let out a breath, which steamed upward in the frosty air much the way the smoke issued from the chimneys all around us. "Surely there must be something else I can do."

Amery shook his head, his expression sober. "Short of taking your case to Lord Greymount, I can't think of what that might be."

Of course. Why hadn't I thought of that?

Phelan Greymount, the lord of Harrow Hall, held sway over Sarisfell and all the lands around it. It was to him that we turned over our tithes, and, after he took his share, he would send the remainder to Tarenmar, to the Mark's exchequer. As our *de facto* intermediary, he was the one I should approach with my suit. Surely he would be able to grant my grandmother and me some form of clemency.

Never mind that I had never laid eyes upon Lord Greymount. He was not one to venture forth from his castle, and so sent his servitors out into the countryside to collect the tax money, and also to ride through the forests and make sure all was well, that Clem did not take more wood than he was allowed, and that the rest of us did not over-hunt the region. Most of the people in Kerolton felt blessed in their absent lord, for it was far better to have one who took not enough interest in his vassals than to have an overlord who meddled in all their daily pursuits.

"That is an excellent notion, Amery," I said, hope beginning to kindle within me. "I shall go to Lord Greymount and plead my case."

His eyes widened in shock. "But you cannot do that, Bettany! For one thing, his castle is more than three leagues hence, far too great a distance for you to walk, especially with this storm coming on."

Once again I looked heavenward, then shrugged. "I see no storm, only grey clouds that have lingered over the forest for the past two days. I do not think I have anything much to fear."

"But Davyn's bad leg has been paining him, a sure sign that snow is coming!"

"I would rather say that Davyn's leg paining him is a sure sign that he didn't wish to chop any more wood." Davyn was Clem Wisegrot's brother-in-law, and a lazier man I was sure I had never seen. He had done well to marry Clem's sister, knowing the family's wealth would keep him from ever having to put in an honest day's work. Instead, he spent most of his time in Hamm's tavern, offering his opinion on the weather and a whole host of other matters he knew very little about. I went on, "It is not yet noon, and if I set out now, I can be there and back before dark."

"You do not know the way."

"No," I admitted. "But there is a clear enough path through the forest, one that leads directly to Lord Greymount's castle. I know where the path lies, even if I have never had need to take it before now. The way is kept open by his lordship's men, so I believe it will be an easy walk."

Amery's mouth set. I could tell he wished to argue further—and I could also tell he was running out of protests to make. As I had pointed out, I was not his daughter. He could not forbid me from going, only tell me how foolhardy my plan was.

"And what if it begins to snow?"

"Then I will walk more quickly," I said calmly. "I daresay Lord Greymount is not such a brute that he would bar me from staying at his home, should the weather require me to do so. Surely a castle must have a spare room or two."

"I fear you do not know much of which you speak," Amery replied. "His lordship does not tolerate visitors."

"Tolerating them and turning them out to die in the cold are two very different things. Not that I believe things will come to such a pass. I will be there and back before anyone knows I am gone."

"So you are not going to tell your grandmother?" There was a hint of desperation in his question, as if Amery had realized the only way to prevent me from setting forth on such a fool-hardy expedition was to appeal to my sense of familial guilt.

"I will lose valuable time if I go back to the cottage," I told him. "For it is the opposite direction from whence I must go. Perhaps you can get word to her somehow?"

A long pause, and then Amery said, his voice heavy, "I will send Evvyn. He still regards a walk in the winter woods as an adventure."

Evvyn was Amery's youngest, a lively boy of nine. He would look on the delivery of such a message as a welcome task, rather than an icy journey with little reward. Well, some reward would be involved, for I was certain my grandmother would give him one of her honey cakes as a gift for delivering the message.

"Thank you, Amery." That was all I said, but he seemed to understand.

"I cannot stop you from doing this, Bettany. But...take care."

"I always do," I said stoutly, then turned from him so I might take the path that led northward out of the village.

To Lord Greymount.

At first, the going was easy enough. True, the air around me was still and cold, biting against the exposed skin of my face, but I was used to winter's chill. At least there was no wind to speak of, nothing I would have to fight against as I made my way through the forest. And yes, perhaps there was the risk of encountering a wild animal, but my grandfather had taught me they were often more afraid of us than we were of them, and if

I walked calmly with a strong, sure step, more often than not any animals I encountered would avoid me and go in search of easier prey.

Besides, ever since Grandfather died, I had worn a long knife on my belt as I went about my business in the forest. That knife served many useful purposes, not the least of which was deterring predators, whether or not they went on four legs or two. Yes, the village was safe enough, as were the lands that surrounded it, but I often had to range far in my searches for dyestuffs, and I had heard rumors that sometimes desperate men would hide within the woods, outlaws seeking to escape the justice of the Mark's guard.

Those rumors had remained just that, for I had never seen anything more frightening than a bear on those foraging missions. It was hard to say who was more startled in that one instance, the bear or I. We had stared at one another for a long moment, and then he turned and ambled away, and a minute or so after that, I remembered to breathe.

So I felt safe enough as I made my way steadily northward. Perhaps it had been foolish to set out with no food or water, but three leagues was really not as far as Amery wished to make it sound. Walking briskly, I should reach Lord Greymount's castle within three hours. Surely they would offer enough hospitality that I would be given water and perhaps a small bite to eat, oatcakes or somesuch.

No, a castle would most likely have something far grander to offer than oatcakes. My imagination rather failed me at that point, for of course I had never seen the inside of a castle, or the outside, for that matter. When Lord Greymount's men came to collect the taxes, or to inspect the woodlands, they did present rather a fine appearance in their doublets of deep blue with the silver wolf's head emblazoned on the breast, and their steel greaves and helmets shining in the sun. But they never stayed, not even to take some porter at Hamm's inn, before returning to their lordship's castle.

Their lordship. What would he be like, our lord of Harrow Hall? I had heard only the barest details of his person, for even the gossips in the village did not have much information to relate. He was not all that old, being some thirty and three years. The title and the castle had gone to him nearly two decades ago, when the former Lord Greymount passed from a fever and left his young son to carry on without him. Ever since Phelan Greymount inherited the lands that had been his father's, we expected to hear that he had taken a noble bride from the court in Tarenmar, so he might carry on the family line, but it seemed his lordship was not disposed to marry, for he was yet without a wife.

Since no one in the village had ever seen him, and because of his apparent reluctance to enter into matrimony, some ugly rumors had swirled about—that he was deformed in some way, that he was so ugly not even his title was enough to make him appealing. I had always brushed those rumors aside, thinking such sentiments spoke more of the ones who traded them than the person they were actually discussing, but now, as I trudged along the muddy path, I could not help wondering if there might be some truth to those rumors.

In that case, his lordship might be very angry at my intrusion.

I swallowed, and told myself not to be so silly. It was far more likely that Lord Greymount was a haughty sort who did not wish to waste his time on commoners such as myself or the rest of the inhabitants of Kerolton. For all we knew, he had a large retinue of courtiers from Tarenmar who feasted nightly in his castle, although one would have thought we'd have heard something of such revels, if they occurred. At the very least, we should have encountered them as they hunted in the woods of Sarisfell, but no such parties were ever seen.

A flake of snow drifted down to the earth before me, and then another. They were soft and feathery, and so fat they looked fluffy enough to stuff a pillow—if they had been made of down and not ice.

Damn. I paused for a moment and squinted up at the sky, which looked far nearer than it had when I'd taken my leave of Amery and set out on this path. More and more flakes began to descend, leaving white flecks on my gaudy cloak and already beginning to dust the bare mud of the path with sugar-frosting traceries.

Well, there was no help for it. I had been walking long enough that I guessed I was closer to Lord Greymount's castle than I was to the village. Turning back was not an option. The best I could do was increase my pace before the snow grew too deep.

Walking faster did help to warm me somewhat, for along with the snow came a thin, biting wind, one that did its very best to penetrate the folds of my cloak and pierce through the bodice and skirt of homespun I wore beneath it. My boots were thick and sturdy, dearly bought this past summer when my old ones gave out completely. Even so, I could still feel the wet and the cold seeping up through their soles and the knitted woolen stockings I had on.

I ignored the discomfort as best I could and kept walking. This certainly wouldn't be the first time I'd gotten wet through from an untimely snowstorm. And though my grandmother had tutted over me on those previous occasions and made me sit by the fire so I might dry out, I had never once caught a cold or an ague from being so thoroughly soaked. She might have commented on my unusual good health, except that it did save her from days or even weeks of worrying. One did not question such luck, but only accepted it as a gift from the gods. Even so, she must be fretting now, knowing that I had been caught out in the snow. I did not know whether to wish that Amery's son Evvyn had delivered his message on time or not. I feared my grandmother would worry even more if she knew I was on my way to Harrow Hall, rather than merely trying to make my way home through familiar woods.

And this storm—it swirled thicker and thicker, obscuring the path before me. True, that narrow opening through the trees helped to guide me even after the muddy route was more or less obscured by falling snow. If I kept to that opening, one which enterprising souls had cleared long before I was born, then I should remain on course.

But then the trees began to thin, and I came out into open country, a region that seemed to be comprised of blowing snow and nothing else. Of course, I knew that was not true, that in fine weather these were probably handsome, rolling hills, but in that moment, I could feel only despair, for I had no true notion of where I should head next.

I stopped where I was, shivering, holding the opening of my cloak closed as tightly as I could to prevent the rising wind from penetrating right through my garments. Much good that did, for the cold seeping up through the soles of my feet was quite bad enough on its own. My hood slipped down, and the wind pulled at my hair, freeing it from the plait I wore down my back. I blinked when the loose strands whipped about, stinging my eyes.

As I stared into the blinding white, I thought I saw a brief flash of light somewhere ahead, and the dark, looming shape of a building before the snow closed in once more.

That had to be Lord Greymount's castle. I couldn't allow myself to consider any other possibility. Now I had a bearing to follow, even if I couldn't see it clearly at the moment. But I had spotted that light, and the edifice which surrounded it. I couldn't let myself believe otherwise, didn't want to think that I might be chasing only an elusive will o' the wisp.

My footsteps dragged as the snow thickened, but I made myself move forward, all my will focused on the light I had seen. It had to be there. It *had* to.

Strangely, the wind seemed to not be quite as chill, its roar somehow muted in my ears. Was the storm lessening? No, the snow appeared to blow around me quite as wildly as it ever had. I could not allow myself to pause and puzzle through the conundrum, however. I had to keep walking, to keep thinking of the shadowy building I had seen for that one brief moment.

No, it really was quite warm. How lovely to be so comfortable, even with the snow falling all around, slowing my footsteps.

I blinked, and reason seemed to assert itself.

No, you are not warm, my mind told me, assuming my grandmother's brisk, sensible tones. *You are freezing, and you will die out here if you do not reach that castle.*

A small whimper escaped my lips. I wanted to be warm. I didn't want to keep walking. Had I ever been this weary before? I couldn't seem to recall. My thoughts were sluggish, slow and torpid as my very footsteps.

My legs gave way, and I stumbled to my knees in the snow, soaking my skirts. But that was better, wasn't it? Anything was better than that interminable walking. Perhaps if I merely lay down for a little while....

No. I had no idea whether I even uttered the word aloud. Something in me was fighting that insidious warmth, forcing me back to my feet. I stumbled forward a few paces, eyes slitted against the driving snow, the ever-increasing wind. In that moment, I had no clear idea where I was even going, only that I must keep moving, keep putting one foot in front of the other.

My outstretched hands collided with something solid and dark. I blinked, and realized that the obstacle in front of me was a great wooden gate, surrounded by stone walls on either side.

Another whimper, this one of shocked relief, escaped my lips. Somehow, against all odds, I had managed to find Lord Greymount's castle.

A dark iron ring hung from the gate. I reached up and grasped the ring with fingers numb even though they were encased in woolen mittens, then let it fall against the weather-scarred wood with a dull *thud*.

No response. Perhaps they had not heard the sound through the howling of the wind. I took hold of the ring and banged it against the gate, over and over, until my strength failed and I sank once more to my knees. I could no longer feel the cold or the wet. No, the snow bank that had piled up against the gates of the keep was soft and welcoming, so much more comfortable than my hard, narrow bed back home. I was so very tired. Only a little sleep....

I shut my eyes, and let the darkness claim me.

Chapter Two

Pain lanced through my fingers and toes, sharp, insistent. I sucked in my breath with a gasp and began to sit up, only to feel a heavy hand against my shoulder, pressing me back down onto a mound of soft pillows. In that moment, I realized I lay in a real bed, not the snow bank where I had collapsed... when? My memories of what exactly had happened were as hazy and indistinct as the snowy landscape outside the window, which had begun to darken with the coming of night.

I blinked, letting the chamber where I lay come into focus around me. The room appeared to be quite large, almost as large as the cottage I shared with my grandmother. A huge hearth of carved stone took up half of one wall, but I couldn't see much more detail than that because of the bed's hangings, which were a faded blue velvet. At least, I assumed they were velvet. I had never actually seen velvet before, had only read about it in books, and had always considered it nearly as mythical as a dragon or a griffin.

Sitting in a chair next to my bed was an old man, his white hair drawn into a severe tail that fell halfway down his back. I assumed he was the one who had pushed me down against the pillows, for despite his obvious years, he sat as straight as some- one half his age, and his shoulders were still broad beneath the dark doublet he wore.

"Where—" I began, then stopped, for the word had come out as barely a croak.

Without replying, he held out a cup of carved bone. It must have contained something warm inside, for I could see wisps of steam curling away from the liquid within and up into the air.

I took the cup from the stranger, glad of its heat against my still aching fingers. Something prevented me from taking a drink, however. In that moment, I realized my sodden cloak and skirt and bodice had been removed, although it seemed I still wore the chemise I'd had on underneath those garments. Even though it appeared that some of my modesty had been preserved, I couldn't help blushing at the thought that this stranger—or perhaps some other of the servants here—had undressed me while I lay near dead from exposure.

So I slanted the man a look from beneath my eyelashes and paused, the cup cradled in both hands.

"It is only warm broth, child," he said. If he'd noticed the way the hot color had flooded my cheeks, he gave no sign of it. "Drink it. You need to restore your strength."

He sounded impatient with me. I noted a certain clarity to his pronunciation, a crispness to the way he formed his words. *Not from here,* I thought. Perhaps from Tarenmar, although that was mere speculation on my part, since I had never actually spoken with anyone from the capital city and had no idea what their accents might sound like.

I lifted the cup to my lips and drank the broth. It was good, hearty and rich, not overly salty. Another sip, and another. After that, I could feel some energy returning to my limbs, could feel the ache at the back of my throat begin to ease itself.

"Where am I?"

He gave me a smile that showed teeth which were far better than I would have expected in someone his age. "You are in Harrow Hall. Was that not your destination? I fear there is not much else to be found in this part of the world."

"It was my destination," I replied. So they had taken me in. And there I had thought that no one had heard my frenzied pounding on the gates.

"And you are?"

"My name is Bettany Sendris. I come from Kerolton."

"Ah." He glanced away from me toward the hearth, but the logs within seemed to be burning briskly, in no need of assistance. "And what is your business here, Bettany Sendris of Kerolton?"

That was the real question, wasn't it? For some reason, I found myself reluctant to confess my poverty to this elegant old man. The terrible moment must come at some point, but I would rather conduct that particular business with the lord of the manor himself, and no one else. "May I ask your own name, sir?"

Another smile. "I am Lorn Merryk, his lordship's steward. I must surmise that it was grim business indeed that brought you out into such a storm."

"It was not snowing when I left Kerolton." A feeble reply, perhaps, but I did not want this dignified-looking man to think that I had intentionally set out in such weather. Only a very great fool would have taken such a risk.

"This storm did seem to grow in strength very quickly. Our apologies for not coming to your rescue sooner—that ring on the gate does tend to bang about a good bit when the wind picks up, and it was not until one of the guards realized it was being struck with some regularity that he came out to investigate. We do not get very many visitors here, you see."

So much for my theory about Lord Greymount regularly entertaining grand guests from Tarenmar. "Do thank that guard for me, Master Merryk," I said.

"I will." He paused for a moment, keen dark eyes seeming to take in every detail of my appearance. The gods only knew what a wreck I must have looked, although I told myself it was foolish to care about such things when I had been on the very brink of death. "But I fear you have not answered my question, Mistress Sendris. Certainly you were not invited here, which leads me to believe that your errand was important enough to overlook such a lack."

It was my turn to hesitate. My fingers tightened around the cup I held. To stall for time, I drained its contents, then extended my hand so Lorn Merryk could take it from me.

Which he did without comment, before rising from his chair so he could go and set the empty cup on a small table a few feet away from the bed. Standing, he appeared a great deal taller than I had imagined, and far more intimidating. He still wore a pleasant enough expression, but something in the set of his mouth told me he would not be all that patient if I continued to evade his questions.

I cleared my throat, then said, "I fear my reason for being here is something intended for Lord Greymount's ears only."

Master Merryk's brows drew together, and I thought I saw a spark of anger in his dark eyes. "His lordship does not grant audiences."

"Ever?" I asked, before I could prevent the word from escaping my lips. So were the rumors true? Was the lord of Harrow Hall so terribly deformed that he would see no one except his own servitors?

"Rarely," the steward allowed. "Certainly not to young women who show up uninvited on his doorstep."

"But—" Whatever happened, I would not beg. I was the interloper here, yes, but that was not reason enough for me to abandon my dignity. These days, it was the only thing I could say was truly mine. "I know I am asking a great deal, Master Merryk. But my reason for being here is of a personal nature, and so I feel that I can only speak of that reason to his lordship...and no one else."

Those words earned me another frown. Then Lorn Merryk let out something of a sigh, barely more than a very slight exhalation. "Very well, Mistress Sendris. You will need some time to recover before you are strong enough to get out of that bed. Rest this night, and perhaps after you have had a good night's sleep, you will reconsider your position."

I knew that a single night of slumber would not cause me to change my mind, but I also did not wish to argue further. Besides, I could tell that even our brief exchange had begun to tire me. My eyelids seemed weighted with weariness; it was with some difficulty that I continued to keep them open. Even so, I managed to push myself up a little higher against the pillows, so I might get a better look outside. A wasted effort, for a deep purple dusk had descended upon the landscape, which was obscured further by blowing snow.

"I fear the storm is truly upon us," Master Merryk said. "Neither you nor anyone else will be going anywhere tonight—or tomorrow, either, if my guess is correct. So sleep, Mistress Sendris, and we will decide what to do with you once morning has come again."

These words were not terribly reassuring, but at least he had made no mention of throwing me out to the mercies of the wild weather. It seemed I was safe here for now, or at least as safe as an unaccompanied young woman could be in a strange place.

I nodded, and murmured something of thanks. After that, the room began to blur as my eyelids slipped shut. Master Merryk let himself out, then closed the door. And once again I fell into darkness—only this time, I thought I had a chance of awakening on the morrow.

Which I did, into a room dimly lit by a single candle sitting on the same small table where Lorn Merryk had set my empty cup of broth. The fire had been expertly banked, which meant either he or someone else had come in while I slept to attend to that task. I found I did not particularly like the idea of someone creeping around in the chamber while I was deep in sleep, but then I scolded myself.

And you would not have particularly liked having the fire die down completely whilst such a storm raged outside, either. So tend to it now, before it dwindles to nothing.

Shivering, I slipped out of the tall bed and made my way over to the hearth. A goodly pile of logs waited in the metal basket there, and I pulled out several and set them in the fireplace, arranging them with the tongs that hung from a little bracket bolted into the wall. Soon enough, warm yellow flames began to lick along the wood, sending a welcome wave of heat into the room.

Now that I had attended to my most immediate need, I turned to survey the chamber where I had been ensconced. My previous impressions of it from the night before held true—it was very large, and held not only the enormous canopied bed where I had slept, but a little sitting area with a divan and a plumply upholstered chair, along with what I guessed must be a writing desk, although I had never seen one before. A matching chair was placed up against the desk.

Heavy velvet curtains covered the windows. I went to the nearest one and pushed the draperies aside. As soon as my eyes took in the scene outside that window, my heart sank. The snow showed no sign of letting up; if anything, the storm appeared to have increased in ferocity overnight, the world beyond almost completely obscured by heavy blowing veils of white. I could make out no details of the landscape. There was no sign of the path I had taken, and nothing of the forest beyond, even though I knew it must be only a mile or so from Lord Greymount's castle.

It seemed that Master Merryk had been correct in his assertion that the storm would prevent me from traveling today. I tried to tell myself that it did not matter, that clearly the steward intended to provide shelter for me for as long as proved necessary, but worry still clutched at my insides. I had come here to state my case, not to be an unwelcome house guest for possibly days at a time.

No, I told myself. *Surely it will not come to that. A storm that is blowing so fiercely will blow itself out in no time. It is entirely possible that you will be on your way by this afternoon.*

Assuming, of course, that Lord Phelan Greymount would even deign to give me an audience.

If he did, then best that I be ready for it. On one wall was an enormous wardrobe, and I went to it, thinking that my clothes must have been hung in there to dry. But when I opened the large carved doors, a jumble of rich color met my wondering eyes. Not the modest brown and rust of the bodice and skirt I had worn on my journey here, but elegant gowns of velvet and silk in all the shades that were far too expensive for me to have ever worked with when I dyed our rough-spun wool, let alone worn—deep blue, and rich purple, and lush green.

As I ran a hand down the sleeve of one gown, I realized that, despite their colors and fabrics, these dresses were cut in a style which had gone out of fashion before I was even born, and did not consist of a boned bodice and matching skirt, but were all one piece, fashioned to skim the body. Had they belonged to the previous occupant of this room?

A knock at the door made me turn around, heart pounding. In that instant, I realized I stood there in my bare feet and my chemise, certainly not a state for receiving visitors. As quickly as I could, I hurried back to the bed so I could draw the covers up over me and hide something of my deshabille.

Not a moment too soon, for Lorn Merryk entered the room, a tray in his hands. On that tray sat what looked like a pasty of some sort, and a chubby brown pot of tea, along with a mug fashioned of the same thick pottery.

"Feeling better this morning?" he inquired as he set the tray down on the table nearest the bed.

"Much," I replied. Since he had already seen me in the chemise and with my hair tumbling over my shoulders, I did not feel quite as shy in his presence as I might have around yet another stranger. Still, I did find it rather odd that the castle's steward would lower himself to wait on me in such a way. I could not admit to any great knowledge of how a castle's household operated, but surely a chambermaid would have been better suited to that particular task?

He poured some tea into the mug and then brought it over to me. "Let us see how this suits you."

I took the mug from him and allowed myself a sip. The liquid was strong, and strange, and yet I thought I could come to enjoy the flavor. "That is tea?" I asked, and then paused, embarrassed. I did not wish for him to think I had been criticizing the drink.

But he only smiled. "Yes, truly tea, brought all the way from Keshiaar. What you are no doubt used to drinking is actually a tisane, a brew of local herbs and flowers."

Well, that was true enough. We often drank mixtures of chamomile and rose hips, or mint and wild licorice. My grandmother had always called it "tea," and so had everyone else I knew, but clearly we had been misinformed. And to think the tea I now drank had come all the way from Keshiaar, that wild, exotic land thousands of leagues to the south and east. Or at least, I believed that was where it lay. I had only seen a map of the continent once, when a tinker passed through the village and had one among his wares. Oh, how I had wished that we had the coin to purchase it, so I might hang it from the cottage wall and pore over it until I had memorized all the strange names of those lands and towns that seemed so very far away.

But of course we could not afford such a frivolity, and the tinker had rolled up the map and stowed it among his things before driving his wagon away from the village. Off to the east, toward Farendon. I recalled that much, even though I could not remember exactly how many miles he would have to travel before he reached that country's borders.

I offered Master Merryk a smile and said, "Thank you. It is very good."

"I'm glad to hear that it pleases you."

His aspect seemed pleasant enough, and so I said, "Forgive me, but have you inquired of his lordship as to whether he will speak with me?"

At once the old man's dark eyes shuttered, and he shook his head. "I told him of your presence here—for of course the lord of the castle should know such things—and of your wish to see him. He said it was not possible, and that you should deliver your message to me so I might pass it on to him."

I had feared such a response, but that did not make Lorn Merryk's words any easier to hear. My fingers tightened around the mug I held. "I know I am but a lowly village girl, and perhaps Lord Greymount feels it is beneath his dignity to speak to me. However, I—"

Master Merryk raised a hand. "His lordship's dignity has nothing to do with it. I told you already that he does not receive visitors." His expression softened, and he went on, "Truly, Mistress Sendris, you need not fear telling me the reason for your journey here. I will bring your concerns to Lord Greymount, and I have no doubt that he will help you if he can."

Oh, so he is willing to help, but not willing to extend the simple courtesy of seeing me face to face? I thought then. I knew better than to say such a thing to the stately old man who stood before me, however. Rather than responding directly, I slanted the steward a sideways look through my eyelashes and said, "I must thank you for such personal attention, Master Merryk. Surely it is not usual that the steward of a castle would bring an uninvited guest her morning meal?"

At that question, his back went rigid. "We have very few servants here. His lordship leads a modest life."

Not even a chambermaid? I thought then, wondering at such austerity. My question must have shown in my face, for Master Merryk spoke again.

"We have no women servants at Harrow Hall. I thought you would be more comfortable if I brought you your breakfast, since we had already met last night. But if you wish for one of the other men to attend you—"

"No, thank you," I said hastily. How odd that they would have no women working in the castle! However, it was not my place to question Lord Greymount's quirks more than I already had. If truly I was the only woman here, then of course it was far more comfortable to have the elderly steward see to my care, rather than a strange man, one who possibly would be younger and not as circumspect around a woman who was far from the protection of her friends and family. "I am honored to have you come and look in on me, Master Merryk."

The faintest twitch of his lips, a twitch which seemed to deepen the lines that ran from his nose to his mouth. "I thought perhaps you might see it that way." He turned so he could retrieve the plate which held the pasty, then laid it on my lap. "I fear my predictions were accurate—the storm shows no sign of letting up."

"Yes, I saw that," I replied.

At once his gaze strayed to the window where I had drawn back the curtains, and from there to the wardrobe, whose doors still stood open. In my haste to scramble back into bed, I had quite forgotten to close the wardrobe back up. "The gowns should fit you, I think."

"Oh, no," I said at once. "I couldn't presume to wear anything so fine."

He shook his head. "You must dress yourself in something, for the garments you were wearing when you came here are quite ruined. I assure you, she who once owned those gowns is long gone, and will not care if someone else has their use."

I didn't know if I should be dismayed that my skirt and bodice had been muddied and stained beyond repair, or excited at the prospect of wearing one of those beautiful dresses. Never in a hundred years could I have imagined that I might be able to dress myself in something suited for the court at Tarenmar—or rather, suited for that court as it might have been some thirty-odd years ago. We did not follow fashion in Kerolton, but even I knew those gowns were several decades out of date.

"'She who once owned them'?" I ventured.

"His lordship's late mother, the gods rest her." An expression of sorrow passed over his face, but he grew stern immediately after. "She has been gone longer than you have been alive, Mistress Sendris, so do not worry that you are overstepping your bounds. And now you should eat that pasty before it is completely cold. I will check on you at midday."

He gave me a slight bow then before heading out the door. As it shut, I caught a glimpse of a corridor of grey stone, with a faded tapestry covering part of the wall in front of the entrance to my room. That single glimpse was all I got, however, and offered very little to tell me of how large the castle really was, or how far that corridor extended.

Perhaps that was all I'd ever get to see, until the storm broke and Master Merryk escorted me from this place. Certainly nothing he had said so far seemed to indicate that I would ever get to see the master of the castle.

I told myself to be patient, then lifted the pasty from its plate and took a bite. It was good, filled with chunks of venison and potato, and with a savory sauce. After that first mouthful, I realized how hungry I really was, and made short work of the rest of it, wishing that the steward had brought two. Perhaps, since there were no other women in the castle, he didn't understand that a young woman could have just as healthy an appetite as a man.

Once I was done, I decided I should do what I could to get myself cleaned up and presentable, just in case Lord Greymount might relent and agree to see me after all. Master Merryk had made no mention of a bath, but there was a basin of water sitting on a stand near the fire, along with some clean cloths. I went over to it and washed my face and neck as well as I could, then opened a drawer in the stand and found a hair-brush and comb.

Since my hair had become quite knotted during my jour-ney to the castle, I knew getting it presentable again would take some effort. I sat down on the stool in front of the dressing table and began working through the tangles. The mirror above the table was age-blackened in spots, but still far better than anything I had to work with back at my grandmother's cottage. I stared at my reflection, gratified to see that my ordeal of the day before didn't appear to have taken any lasting toll. True, I looked a little pale, but my dark eyes had no shadows beneath them, and the color had returned to my lips, which had always been naturally rosy pink.

Once my hair lay smooth and glossy over my shoulders—in truth, it had never looked so fine, as I had never before had the luxury to groom it so thoroughly with such a good brush—I got up from the dressing table and went to inspect the gowns in the wardrobe. The most elegant of them all was a dress of dark blue velvet with silver embroidery and a collar of soft white fur, but I didn't quite have the courage to put it on. Instead, I reached for a gown made of finely woven dark green wool and pulled it out, draping it over one arm. In a drawer at the bottom of the wardrobe, I found neatly folded chemises and other underthings, cut more narrowly than I was used to because of the form-fitting nature of the gowns they must be worn beneath.

A few sprigs of lavender fell from the folds of a chemise as I shook it out, and the delicate scent wafted up to my nose. I breathed it in, thinking of warmer days when those flowers would bloom. But summer was months away, and I had to focus on my rather dire present. What I tried very hard not to think about was my grandmother's worry over my fate. She must be distressed beyond measure, since of course she had no way of knowing that I had reached Harrow Hall safely, and was now enjoying its hospitality. I could only hope she fared as well as I did, and utter a silent thank-you to the gods that at least we had a good store of wood at hand, since one had been dropped off at the cottage only a few days earlier.

Getting into the gown proved more difficult than I had thought it would be, since it laced up the back. Clearly, it had been intended for a wearer with lady's maids to help her with such tasks, but I had no such assistance. What I did have was plenty of time, and after struggling with the laces for what seemed like at least a half-hour, I got myself more or less securely fastened into the dress. I could only hope that getting out of it wouldn't be quite as arduous an endeavor.

On the floor of the wardrobe were several pairs of slippers. They were slightly large, but since they also laced on, I managed to tie them tightly enough that I thought I should be able to keep them attached to my feet.

Not that walking in them would be much of a problem, considering that it seemed as if I wouldn't be leaving this chamber anytime soon. Master Merryk had said he would be back to check on me at midday, but I had no idea how long that might be.

Once again I went to the window, but although the world seemed marginally lighter, telling me it was later in the day, the sun was obscured by pale grey clouds, and the snow continued to fall. Indeed, it was very difficult to discern where the sky stopped and the storm began, or where the ground even lay.

Because my grandmother had taught me to be neat, I went and made up the bed, and then placed my empty mug and plate next to the little teapot on its table. After that, I folded my discarded chemise and other underthings, and slid them into an empty drawer in the wardrobe.

This industry was all very well and good, but it did not take up a great deal of time. I found myself wishing that the former inhabitant of the room had left some discarded needlework behind. Not that I was anything close to an expert at embroidery—it was far too time-consuming and frivolous, compared to the necessary tasks of darning and sewing and weaving—but at least I could have filled the empty hours with improving my skill at the Selddish knot, or the silk stitch.

Sometime later—how much later, I did not know—Master Merryk appeared with my luncheon, which was a hearty venison stew. I began to guess that Lord Greymount's men did a good deal of hunting when the weather permitted.

"So," the steward said, after giving my freshened appearance a single appraising look, "you do look much improved, Mistress Sendris. Perhaps now that you have had time for reflection, you would allow me to take a message to his lordship?"

I hesitated. Truly, did it make that much of a difference? I could not claim to know Lorn Merryk at all well, but so far he had comported himself like an honorable man. I doubted that he would mock my poverty, or refuse to disturb Lord Greymount with such a frivolous request.

And yet...something inside me balked. I had fought my way through a blizzard to talk to the lord of Harrow Hall, and I did not want to admit defeat now and settle for using an intermediary. However, I also did not want to offend this dignified old man. I wrestled inwardly for a moment, but then decided I must press my case, no matter what the steward might think of my stubbornness.

"I am afraid that is not possible," I said. "My request is of such a personal nature that I feel I cannot in good conscience speak to anyone about it except Lord Greymount."

It seemed Master Merryk had been expecting such a reply, for he did not appear terribly surprised. "I am sorry to hear that."

"And I am sorry to impinge on your hospitality. That was certainly not my intention when I came here."

A nod, and he looked toward the window. I had left the curtains open, although the scene outside had not changed over the intervening hours. The snow fell as heavily as ever. I wondered if it had yet begun to block any of the ground-floor windows, for the drifts must have been feet high by that point.

"Do not worry yourself on that account, mistress. At least you are safe here, and warm." A shadow seemed to pass over his face, and he added, "But have you no family who will be worried on your account?"

A pang went through me at his question, for I knew my grandmother must be in quite a state by now, even though I had done my best to push my worries aside. But still, to be missing overnight, with no way of sending her word that I was safe! It was a terrible thing, but I had no way of remedying the situation. "My grandmother," I replied. "I sent word to let her know I had set forth for Harrow Hall, but that is all she knows."

"Poor woman." To my surprise, the steward laid a comforting hand on my shoulder and gave me a single pat. "She must be worried terribly for you, but imagine her joy when you return home safe and unharmed."

A joy that would be even greater if I could somehow manage to work out an arrangement with Lord Greymount. Such an outcome seemed to be quite the impossibility at the moment, given that he wouldn't even see me.

But I summoned a smile, and soon after Master Merryk went away.

The storm raged on that night, and the morning that followed. And still the snow fell, and the wind howled, although all was warm and safe within. My worry increased with each passing hour. Surely by now my grandmother must think me dead, for no one could live in this weather, and she had no way of knowing that I had reached the castle and was now housed within, enjoying a life of comfort I had never known before.

Because my meals were brought to me, and a warm bath that second day as well. The long hours with nothing to do were the worst of it, but I made do as I could, thinking of how I might repay Lord Greymount if I could get him to agree to my plan, and tidying the room, and sitting at the window and watching the snow pile ever higher. I never saw anyone leave the castle—not that I expected them to. Even a strong man on a stronger horse would not survive for very long in that maelstrom. I could not recall ever seeing a storm of such ferocity, or such duration. Old Hamm, who owned the tavern, sometimes spoke of a devil storm that had swept over North Eredor before I was even born, a storm that had frozen the River Elskar solid and covered the land in so much snow that people froze in their homes, and the ice persisted in the shadows of trees and walls until almost midsummer.

I had always thought him to be exaggerating. Now I could only worry that such a storm had come again.

Despite the drafts that leaked in past the casement, I sat at the window, watching the snow blow past. Indeed, it seemed almost a living thing, that if I only looked closely enough, I could see shapes writhing and forming in those blowing curtains of ice.

A knock came at the door, and I started. Then I rose to my feet. "Come in," I said, although I found myself wondering at the timing of this visitor. It was not yet dark enough outside for Master Merryk to be bringing me my supper.

He entered, but waited just inside the doorway. "Mistress Sendris," he said, quite formally.

For some reason, my heart began to beat more quickly. "Yes, Master Merryk?"

Although I thought I had begun to learn something of his expressions during the past few days, I could see nothing in his features in that particular moment to inform me of the purpose of this visit. But then he said, "His lordship will see you now."

Chapter Three

It was a good thing that my hand rested on the back of the chair where I had been sitting, for I needed it to steady myself. "His lordship...?" I faltered.

"He has decided that he will speak with you." For the first time, a tiny glint entered Lorn Merryk's eyes. "That is, if you still wish to speak to him."

"Of course," I said, doing my best to recover from my shock. "That is—that is very kind of him."

"Ah, well." These two syllables were accompanied by a lift of the steward's shoulders. "He has decided that he wants to see for himself the young woman who has exhibited such a display of will."

That, I feared, was a polite way of putting it. As my grandmother had often lamented, I did possess a strong stubborn streak. It was not that I ever intended to be willful, more that I tended to find myself wondering why others did not see the common sense of my own wishes.

But no matter. Lord Greymount had asked for me, and that was the important thing. Unconsciously, I reached up to smooth my hair, then looked down to make sure the belt of linked brass medallions I wore was not hanging askew.

Master Merryk waited near the door, a faint smile on his lips. Perhaps he thought me vain for making sure I would be presentable for my meeting with his lordship. I did not think that vanity had much to do with it. Rather, I did not want to appear like some disheveled village girl in front of such a grand lord, especially when I must ask him to grant me such a very large favor.

Hoping that I would pass muster, I went to the steward. "I am ready."

"This way, mistress."

For the first time since my sojourn in the castle began, I stepped outside my door. As that one fleeting glimpse had told me, the corridor was constructed of grey stone, with tapestries—some fairly bright and new, others worn and faded—hanging at more or less regular intervals. The floor in my room was covered in rugs from Keshiaar and other exotic locales, but beneath my feet here was only bare stone, chilly through the thin soles of the borrowed slippers I wore.

We traversed that hallway and came to a great stone staircase. Master Merryk led me up one flight of steps, then another. I began to wonder how large the castle truly was. In that moment, I rather thought that every house in Kerolton—even Master Wisegrot's two-story home—could have fit quite neatly inside Harrow Hall.

But after climbing yet another set of stairs, we came to a large landing. On the left side was a pair of double doors, carved with the shapes of twining branches and flying birds. Hawks, they looked like.

Master Merryk rapped smartly on that door, then called out, "I have her here, my lord."

A pause, followed by a deep voice saying, "Have her come in."

Something about that voice sent a small chill down my back. Perhaps it was simply that Lord Greymount had rather taken on the aspect of a mythical creature during the past few days, and so hearing him speak startled me, made me realize he truly was a living man. Also, now that it had come time to beard the lion in his den, so to speak, an understanding of the depths of my audacity came over me. Who was I, a simple girl from Kerolton, to demand that the lord of Harrow Hall listen to my requests?

Too late to turn back now, unfortunately. Master Merryk pushed the door open and said, "Go on."

I turned beseeching eyes upon him. "You will not see me in?"

"His lordship wishes to see you alone." Tone gentle, he added, "Was this not what you wished for?"

Well, it was. I could not show any hesitation now, not after my former intransigence. I nodded at the steward, then walked past him and through the doorway. As soon as I was inside, I heard the door shut behind me.

Like the rest of the castle, this suite—for it must be a suite, as I saw more doors opening off a short corridor—had been constructed of grey stone. The effect was somewhat livelier here, however, for all the tapestries appeared to be in good repair. Likewise, the rugs beneath my feet glowed with rich colors of crimson and dark blue and deep green.

The hallway I traversed opened into a large room, much larger than the bedchamber I had occupied for the past few days, although that space had seemed inordinately oversized for just one person to inhabit. At one side was a large hearth of stone carved into motifs similar to those that had decorated the door to the suite, of flying birds and graceful branches, while a row of windows had been cut into the wall directly ahead of me. Silhouetted against one of those windows was the tall figure of a man.

He turned as I entered the room, and I had to keep myself from catching my breath. Oh, no, he was not deformed at all. Rather the opposite. I had to admit to myself that my experience was not terribly large, but I knew I had never seen a more handsome man. His heavy dark hair swept back from his brow, and his eyes were equally dark, piercing under his black brows. Some might have argued that his nose was too long, or perhaps his lips somewhat thin, but the combination of all those features was quite enough to take my breath away—especially when I had been expecting something so very different.

"Mistress Sendris, I presume?" he inquired, the ironic flip at the end of his question telling me that he was not overly impressed by my behavior.

I nodded and moved forward a few steps. From that spot in the center of the room, I could feel the heat from the fire, far larger and more impressive than the one I'd left burning in my bedchamber. "Yes, my lord. Thank you so much for agreeing to see me—"

"Yes, that," he cut in, clearly having little use for my pleasantries. "You gave me little choice, it seems."

Color flooded my cheeks. Oh, why had I been so stubborn? Standing there, and having him look at me with that sardonic tilt to his eyebrows, quite made me want to melt into the floor. But since I had come here on this errand, I must see it through to its conclusion, no matter what Lord Greymount might say... and no matter how he might say it.

"I am sorry for that, my lord. But I do believe that when you hear why I have come here, you will understand why I did not wish to confide in Master Merryk."

"Indeed? That sounds rather dire." Lord Greymount gestured toward a table a few feet away from him, one on which several costly goblets of cut glass and a matching decanter sat. "Perhaps you should have a drink with me first, to give you courage."

I had never drunk spirits—or wine—in my life. Cider, of course, and a small mug of ale at the village's Midwinter celebration, but nothing more than that. Still, I did not want his estimation of me to go any lower than it already had...if that was even possible. "Thank you, my lord. That sounds lovely."

A knowing smirk played around the edges of his mobile lips, but he said nothing, only went over to the table and poured a measure of deep, ruby-colored liquid into each of the goblets. He then handed one to me, and I took it, praying that I wouldn't drop the precious glass. Surely it had to be worth more than everything my grandmother and I owned.

"To communication," he said, raising his goblet.

I raised mine as well, then allowed myself a very small sip. What passed over my tongue was unlike anything I had tasted before—redolent of raisins, but sweeter, richer. My eyes widened, but I somehow kept myself from taking another, larger swallow. I needed to keep my wits about me, and I could tell that the liquor, whatever it might be, was far stronger than anything I'd ever drunk before.

From the slight narrowing of Lord Greymount's eyes, I could tell that he had noticed my reaction. But he forbore from commenting, and said only, "Will you not sit, Mistress Sendris?" With his free hand, he indicated one of two chairs upholstered in cut velvet that flanked the small table where the decanter sat.

"Oh, I couldn't possibly—"

"I fear I must insist."

The steel in his tone propelled me forward, and I seated myself with some reluctance. Certainly I had never thought to find myself sitting in his lordship's presence, but his invitation had not left any room for protest.

A moment later, he sat as well, then poured himself some more of the ruby liquid. This close, he really was quite overwhelming. I couldn't help but breathe in the warm, spicy scent that seemed to emanate from the doublet of dark wool he wore, or notice the breadth of his shoulders and the strength of his legs as he stretched them out before him. Truly, I had never seen a man like him before. He made even Vianna Willar's handsome betrothed look like a pale, weak thing.

But I could not allow myself to become distracted. I had no idea if his lordship could detect his effect on me, and I resolved not to let that matter, one way or another. At the moment, he seemed more amused than annoyed, and while I did not particularly enjoy being seen as a source of amusement, better that than to have him angry with me.

I did take another very small sip of the wine—or whatever it was—before speaking. "Again, my lord, I must thank you for your patience with me. I never intended to trespass on your hospitality in such a way."

"No, probably not," he agreed, gaze shifting to the ever-blowing snow outside the window before returning to me. "That, I suppose, is in the hands of the gods, and they don't generally do very well at explaining themselves."

Better to overlook that casual blasphemy. I had never heard anyone criticize the gods before, but then, I had never before been in the presence of a nobleman. Perhaps they were allowed license not given to commoners.

Because he was watching me with some expectation, I knew I could not waste more time with pleasantries, or apologies for the way I had more or less stranded myself here. I folded my hands in my lap, then said, "My lord, it embarrasses me to make this request of you, but I have no other recourse. This month, and the autumn which preceded it, were a very difficult time for my grandmother and myself. We—"

"What of your husband?" his lordship interrupted. He glanced at my left hand, which was quite bare, but I knew that did not necessarily indicate an unmarried status. Many of the men in Kerolton did not have the means to purchase a ring for their wives.

"I have no husband."

Lord Greymount's eyebrows lifted at that revelation, as if he did not quite believe me. For some reason, I found his astonishment rather gratifying. Did he think me fair, and wonder why no man had yet claimed my hand?

But that was foolishness on my part. I was so far beneath a man such as Phelan Greymount as to be nigh invisible. More likely that he was surprised to find a young woman of the advanced age of twenty-one to be unmarried. Most of the girls in my village were wed and mothers by the time they were eighteen. I, on the other hand, was not seen as suitable by most of the men of Kerolton, with a mother who had disappeared into the forest when her child was not even three years old, and a father who had never been named. I bore the name of my mother, and her family, and not the man who had sired me, for no one knew who he was.

Yet another secret my mother had taken with her when she vanished.

"Ah," said Lord Greymount, after a rather awkward pause. "Then it seems the men of your village must be blind, but we will leave that aside for now. You were speaking of a difficult autumn?"

Once again my cheeks flushed, but I ignored that obvious sign of my embarrassment and said, "Yes. We had to repair the roof of our cottage, and a wolf got Sissi—"

"Sissi?"

"Our goat."

"Unfortunate."

Oh, he was laughing at me, wasn't he? More than ever I wished I could take the goblet he'd given me and drain its contents, so I might gain some much-needed courage from the strong liquor. I ignored the impulse, however, and went on, "We are not rich, my lord. Much of what we do is in barter, but we cannot barter to pay our taxes."

At that word, he seemed to stiffen. "So that is what this is all about?"

I experienced a sinking sensation somewhere in my midsection, for his tone had grown quite cool. "Yes, my lord. I came here to beg for clemency, to ask if you would but extend us some credit for a few months. Just—just until the summer comes again, and I am able to gather the materials I need for my dyes. Once I am able to sell more fabric for ready coin, then I would be able to repay you."

Silence. He regarded me carefully for a moment, then got up from his chair and went to the window. I was not sure whether I should follow him or not, so I remained seated where I was, fingers knotted around one another in my lap. Despite the relative warmth of the room, those fingers felt to me cold as ice, chill as the frozen world outside.

Still staring out at that frigid landscape, Lord Greymount said, "And what would you have me do, Mistress Sendris? For the Mark expects his measure from his lords, whether or not the tenants of those lords pay their fair share."

"I—" It seemed wrong to be speaking to him like that over my shoulder, so I rose from my seat and went over to the window as well. It was much colder there, and I had to fight to keep myself from shivering. "I know it is a great deal to ask. I do not like to make an exception of myself, but I had no other choice."

He didn't move. The wintry light streamed over his features, accenting the long, elegant sweep of his nose, the determined jut of his chin.

No, you shall not admire him, I told myself fiercely. *It is clear that he is about to refuse you, even though the sum involved is probably less than the cost of one of his boots.*

Then he did turn toward me. I saw no softening in the lines of his mouth, and I braced myself. Would he also throw me out in the snow after he had refused my request? No, that was a foolish notion. He could have done that days ago if he had been so inclined.

"How much?" he asked.

My cold fingers knotted themselves in the warm woolen folds of my borrowed gown. "T-two silver pieces, my lord."

"A staggering sum, to be sure."

He was mocking me. I repressed the urge to snap at him, to tell him that what might seem like nothing to him was a great deal to me, to my grandmother. Instead, I stood there in silence, knowing there was nothing I could say to sway him. I did not know this man, but I could already tell that he was not one who had much patience for begging or pleading.

Then he said, "Tell me, Mistress Sendris. What would you do for those two silver pieces?"

"'Do'?" I repeated, puzzled.

"Yes, do. Surely you do not expect me to give you those two silver pieces in exchange for nothing?"

I tilted my chin up at him. "I already told you, my lord, that I would repay the sum in a few months, after I have time to replenish my stock and sell some of my goods."

"Ah, that. There are some who would say that summer is a good deal more than just a 'few' months off, but rather half the year. Do you intend to pay interest on this loan, since it will extend for such a lengthy amount of time?"

Interest? What in the world was he talking about? "I fear I do not understand, my lord."

"Forgive me. I forget that you are a simple girl from a small village." I stiffened, but made myself stand calm and still as he continued, "'Interest,' Mistress Sendris, is a small percentage of the original sum of the loan, a sort of tax for taking your time to pay it back. So on your two silver pieces, if we were going to ask for interest of ten percent, that would be twenty copper pieces in addition to the two silver you originally borrowed."

My head swam. So if he would deign to lend me the two silver, I would also have to give him twenty copper pieces? I had never before heard of such a thing. It sounded like outright theft to me, but I knew I didn't dare tell his lordship that. "I—I see."

"I am not sure that you do, but that is no matter. If I lend you the money to cover your taxes, do you promise that you will repay me with interest?"

So he was not going to deny me outright. Could I come up with such a staggering sum? Perhaps, if I could convince more of my fellow villagers to pay me with real coin, and not a dozen eggs or a sack of meal or whatever else people tended to use for currency in our part of the world. What would happen if I could not repay him?

Then you will go to the debtor's gaol, just as you feared at the beginning. But at least you will have held off the evil day for a six-month, which is something. Much can happen in the span of six months.

I looked up into his eyes. In the pale light that shone through the many-paned windows, it seemed almost as if there was a spark of gold behind the darkness of his irises. But I knew that strange shimmer must have been only a trick of the light.

"I promise," I said, praying that my oath might not turn out to be a lie.

"Then we must shake on it," he said, and extended a hand.

Something in me quailed at having to touch him in such a way, flesh to flesh—it seemed far too intimate—but I knew there was nothing I could do to avoid the contact. Besides, it was only a simple handshake, the ancient way to honor such a deal. I need not make a fuss about it.

I reached out my right hand and felt his fingers wrap around mine. In that moment, it was as if a spark kindled between us. A strange, pulsing warmth rushed from my palm and up into my arm, and I snatched my hand away.

Lord Greymount was staring down at me, eyes wide with consternation. "Who are you?" he asked after a weighty pause, the elegant timbre of his voice somehow gone ragged.

"I—I'm no one, my lord." That was true enough. I was a woman without parents, without wealth, without a name.

For a long moment, he said nothing, but only stood there, clenching and unclenching the hand I had touched. I could see the way his breast rose and fell as he pulled in a breath. Was he angry with me? What I had done?

"Go," he said then. "Get out of my sight."

I couldn't move. It was if some strange force held me rooted in place, standing only a pace away from him.

Then I did see a flash of true anger in his eyes, shining gold and orange and red. But no, that had to be a reflection from the fire.

"Go!" he roared, and suddenly I had the strength to move away from him, to run down the corridor of his suite and out into the larger hallway. The air there was much colder, chilling me to my very core. I began to shiver as I hurried back to my chamber.

And yet I knew my trembling had very little to do with the unheated corridors of Harrow Hall.

~ Chapter Four ~

I thought I knew the way. After all, it had seemed so simple when Master Merryk brought me to Lord Greymount's chambers. I only had to descend three flights of stairs, and then go down a long hallway until I came to the fourth door on the left, which was the entrance to my borrowed room.

Only when I tried to open that door, I found it locked. I rattled the handle, but it would not budge. Tears of anger and frustration stung my eyes, but I would not let them fall. Bad enough that Phelan Greymount would dismiss me in such a way. But to be found sobbing outside the door to my room? It wasn't to be borne.

Not there seemed to be much chance of discovery. The hall around me was empty. In truth, I hadn't heard a whisper of anyone else in the castle besides Master Merryk and Lord Greymount himself. Was it only the two of them in this great grey pile? No, that couldn't be right. The steward had told me that there were no women servants, but he'd intimated that there was some sort of household staff. At any rate, I knew the lord of Harrow Hall employed men-at-arms, for I myself had seen them riding through the forest from time to time.

I couldn't stand in this corridor forever. It appeared I must go in search of Master Merryk so that he might guide me back to my room. Yes, by doing so, I could get myself even more lost. On the other hand, I didn't really see how much more lost I could be than I already was. At any rate, going in search of the steward would offer me some much-needed distraction. I couldn't forget the strange heat which had flooded up my arm when I touched Phelan Greymount's hand. Never in my life had I ever experienced such a thing.

And that strange flash of hot color in his eyes?

No, that must have been my imagination, brought on by the shock of what I had felt.

Who are you? he had demanded, as if I hid some terrible secret from him. But I was hiding nothing, although much had been hidden from me throughout my life.

My hands shook, and I buried them in the folds of my borrowed skirt, glad that I had been offered that much hospitality. The gowns in the wardrobe were not only grand, but warm as well.

Still clenching my skirts, I turned away from the door where I'd stood and went to the landing, then looked down the hallway in the opposite direction. It did not look familiar at all, with a runner of muddy-colored weave covering the center of the floor. I would not waste my time going that way.

It seemed that down was the best direction to go. Perhaps I had miscounted the number of flights we had actually climbed, and I still had to descend one more to reach my borrowed chamber. But when I went to the door I thought might be mine, again it was locked—as were all the others in that corridor.

Abandoning any caution I might have possessed, I tried every door in that hallway, only to find them all shut against me. No one came out to demand what I was doing, and so I truly began to think my wild theory had been true, and that no one inhabited this enormous building save the man who owned it and his lone servitor.

Well, even if that happened to be the case, it still meant that Master Merryk must be about somewhere. Jaw clenched in determination, I descended the stairs once again, this time going directly to the ground floor. As I neared the bottom, I hesitated, for at last I did hear the murmur of men's voices, more than I had ever thought I had heard gathered in a single place. Once again, my hands began to tremble, but I told myself to be brave, that I was still Lord Greymount's guest, even if he had dismissed me so rudely. Besides, perhaps one of the men I now heard could direct me to my room.

I emerged into a great hall with a lofty ceiling of alternating carved beams and flat panels of dark wood. At the far end of that hall was a fireplace so large that it seemed as if entire tree trunks burned within it. Clustered near that fireplace, sitting at a long table with benches on either side, was a group of about twenty men wearing the dark blue wool doublets, trimmed in grey, that I recognized as the livery of his lordship's household. Here in the castle, they had apparently abandoned the steel greaves and helmets they donned when they rode through the forest on official business.

As one, they turned and looked at me when I began to make my gingerly approach. A murmur swept over them, but I could not make out what they were saying. Everything in me was telling me to turn around and head back up the stairs. That was foolishness, though, or at the very least a nervousness I needed to ignore. Certainly I was safe enough here.

One of the men stood and came toward me. As he grew closer, I could see that he was probably of an age with his lordship, and therefore in his early thirties. The resemblance ended there, however, for while this man was also dark-haired, his eyes were a pale, restless blue, and a jagged scar marred one of his cheeks. That scar seemed to move of its own accord as he grinned at me, pulling his expression into something resembling an exaggerated grimace.

"Well, and who are you, my lady?" he asked.

I hesitated, uncertain as to whether he knew very well who I was, and so mocked me with that "my lady," or whether he truly had no idea who I was, and so gave me the honorific because of the rich garments I wore. But my grandmother had always said it was better to expect the best of people, rather than the opposite, and so I said, "My name is Bettany Sendris, sir. I am a guest here in Lord Greymount's castle."

Something in my reply apparently amused him, because he threw his head back and laughed. Discomfited by his reaction, I glanced past him to see what his companions were doing. They all had remained seated, but I could tell that they watched our exchange with some interest.

"Indeed?" the man said, once he had recovered himself. "That is an interesting tale, my lady, for you must know that no woman has graced the halls of this castle for almost two decades."

My first response was to say that he must be mistaken, but I held my tongue. Surely he knew better than I who or who not had been here during Harrow Hall's past. Still, my mind reeled at what he had just told me. Truly, had not a single woman set foot here for almost as long as I had been alive? What on earth could be the reason for such a strange omission?

"That may be," I said, hoping the man-at-arms hadn't noted the way I paused before answering. "As I have never been here before, I cannot say one way or another. All I know is that his lordship offered me shelter from the storm."

"It's true," offered another of the men, who had approached while I was speaking with the first man-at-arms. "Heard her banging on the gate and fetched Master Merryk. Near dead she was."

"She doesn't look dead now," said the first man-at-arms, giving me a leer. Or at least, it appeared to be that sort of look. The scar on his cheek tended to twist all his expressions. "And why did you not tell the rest of us about her, Lewyn?"

"Because Master Merryk told me not to, that's why," Lewyn responded. He seemed somewhat older than the man-at-arms with the scarred face, perhaps as much as forty, with laugh lines bracketing his bright blue eyes and a few flecks of grey in his dark hair.

My lips parted. I wished to thank him for his kindness in hearing me and bringing me inside and out of the storm, but I did not have the opportunity, for the other man-at-arms spoke again.

"Don't see why she had to be such a secret."

If the way the scarred man kept looking at me was any indication, I thought I could guess why the steward had wished to conceal my presence here. Since Lewyn, the older man, seemed far more sympathetic, I addressed my next words to him. "Do you know where Master Merryk is? I fear I cannot find my way back to my chambers, and so that is why I have come in search of him."

Lewyn began to reply, but the scarred man overrode him, saying, "Surely you don't want to go back into hiding quite so soon, pretty lady? Come and sit with us by the fire. There's warm cider."

The very last thing I wanted to do was go and sit anywhere with him. True, Lewyn seemed steady enough. But still, I was a woman alone, and the thought of being surrounded by men I didn't know quite unnerved me. "I—I thank you for your kind invitation," I said. "But I think it is better if I go back upstairs. I am sure if I retrace my steps, I shall be able to find my room."

"And hide yourself away? That would be quite the waste, now, wouldn't it?"

He laid a hand on my arm, fingers encircling my wrist. I wanted to jerk away from his grasp, but feared that doing so would only cause more of a scene. Lewyn seemed distressed on my behalf, but not enough that he apparently intended to intercede. Was the scar-faced man his superior, even though he was clearly younger?

A wave of cold air entered the hall, causing the fire to flicker. Despite the man-at-arm's grip on my wrist, I turned to see the source of that cold blast, and realized it had come from

Lorn Merryk entering through a side door, one that possibly led to the castle's courtyard. Snow thickly coated the hood and shoulders of the dark cloak he wore. My attention, however, was caught by his two companions: a pair of great white dogs, their coats quite as snowy as the world outside. They looked at me with keen golden eyes, then shook mightily, flinging bits of snow in all directions.

"What is this?" Master Merryk demanded.

At once the scar-faced man-at-arms let go of my wrist. "Nothing at all, Master Merryk. It seems Mistress Sendris here lost her way, and we were only trying to put her to rights."

The steward's keen dark gaze flicked toward me. "Is this true? Are you lost, mistress?"

That much I could admit to. "I confess I am. When I was finished speaking with Lord Greymount"—there was a nice understatement!—"I retraced my steps to my room, but I must not have been paying as close attention as I thought to the route, for I did find myself in an unfamiliar part of the castle. So I came down here, as I heard voices and thought I might find someone to assist me."

"Well, I can take you up," Master Merryk said. The dogs he held pulled at their leads and came over to me, sniffing curiously at my skirts. One of them pushed his snout against my hand and whined faintly. I began to scratch his ears, and his eyes shut in ecstasy. "Now, that's odd," the steward commented, even as he gave a stern look at the two men who had been standing next to me. They both slipped away to join their companions near the fire—but not before the scar-faced man gave me a last, lingering glance.

I repressed the urge to shudder, instead saying, "What is odd, Master Merryk?"

"Doxen and Linsi," he replied with a nod toward the two dogs, who were now both getting their ears scratched, one to each of my hands. Not that I minded; their soft, warm fur felt marvelous against my cold fingers. "They're not known to take to strangers."

"Ah, well," I said, bending down so I could better reach their ears. "I am not precisely a stranger, am I? For I have been staying here in the castle for almost three days now. Perhaps they were already used to my scent."

"Perhaps." Master Merryk still looked troubled, however. But then I saw his shoulders lift slightly, and he went on, "Let me take you back to your room, Mistress Sendris. And then I will bring you your supper."

Both of those things sounded wonderful to me. Privacy, and some food. Perhaps then I would be able to gather my wits and attempt to analyze precisely what had passed between Lord Greymount and myself.

So I nodded, and the steward led me from the hall. Before we went, however, he undid the dogs' collars from their leads, and they bounded ahead of us, as if they were determined to be the ones to guide me back to my chamber. And indeed, perhaps my comment about them knowing my scent had some merit, for they did go unerringly to a room on the third floor and stop in front of its doorway, tails wagging.

"They are very beautiful animals," I said as Master Merryk opened the door for me. "Are they yours?"

"Oh, no," he replied. "They are Lord Greymount's—I was taking them for their evening constitutional. Which, I fear, wasn't much, because of the weather. But they are bearing up quite well, all things considered."

It was on my tongue to ask tartly whether his lordship was above exercising his own dogs—but then I realized that of course he was. Even in as small a household as this, someone like Phelan Greymount would have someone to cook his meals, wash his linens, mop the floors—and oversee his dogs' care and feeding. "So you are taking them back up to him?"

"Yes, now that I've seen you safely here." Master Merryk's expression grew exasperated, and he said, "Doxen, come!"

For the dog had pushed past me and was nosing contentedly around my chamber. He sent a glance in our direction and came trotting over, pink tongue lolling happily from his mouth as if he hadn't a care in the world.

"It's quite all right," I reassured him. Truly, I would have been happy to have those dogs stay with me for a while. It would be quite difficult to feel alone when blessed with such companions. My grandmother and I could not afford to feed a dog, although we had a cat to keep the mouse population down. One would have thought my grandfather would have a dog to help him with his hunting, but every dog he'd ever met made him sneeze quite violently, and so we'd done without. I'd often wished to have a dog of my own, having watched with some envy other families in the village who had as many as two or three.

Master Merryk hesitated then, looking from me down to the two magnificent animals. I wondered if he meant to ask me how my interview with Lord Greymount had gone, and what on earth I should say if he did. But instead he gave me a nod, saying, "Well, I'd best be upstairs. His lordship will be wondering where his companions are. And then I'll see to your dinner, mistress."

He headed toward the staircase, the dogs trotting amiably at his heels. I was struck by a sudden image of Lord Greymount bending down to stroke them, those long, sun-browned fingers of his half-buried in their luxuriant white fur. In that moment, I thought it might be quite a good thing to be a dog, if it meant getting to revel in such caresses.

Then I shook my head, and told myself not to be such a fool. Considering the way we had parted, I doubted very much that I would ever be on the receiving end of Phelan Greymount's caresses.

I slept restlessly that evening. My previous two nights in the castle, I had enjoyed more or less uninterrupted slumber, but try as I might, I couldn't seem to find a comfortable position in my borrowed bed. Which seemed silly, considering how its feathery, downy softness was far more luxurious than the straw mattress, suspended by ropes, that I slept on at home. No, I feared the bed was not at fault here.

Perhaps it was only the memory of his lordship's hand in mine, the heat I had experienced—and which he had obviously felt as well.

Who are you? he had asked, and I still wasn't sure how I would answer, if he should ever deign to speak to me again.

To all outward appearances, I was no one very special at all. My mother had apparently been the village beauty—not that such an accolade was terribly difficult to acquire in a hamlet as small as Kerolton—and my grandmother always said I resembled her greatly, although she had blue eyes, like most of the people of North Eredor, while mine were as dark as my hair.

My father's eyes? Most likely, but no one had ever seen him to tell me one way or another. My mother had gotten with child on a midsummer night when she was barely eighteen, and refused to tell anyone who had dishonored her. Privately, I suspected someone passing through, a tinker or traveling merchant, while my grandmother believed the man in question must have been one of the former Lord Greymount's men-at-arms.

I always considered that possibility to be wishful thinking on her part, for such a man could have been compelled to give me his name, as well as some form of monetary support. But no one had been able to prove his identity one way or another, and once my mother was gone, well, the truth of the matter went with her.

Most of the time, I did not care. My grandfather stepped in to help take care of me, and I had never found myself lacking a man's influence while growing up. After he was gone...well, that was more difficult. I somehow doubted Master Wisegrot would have been quite so insulting in his proposal to me— offering to take me off my grandmother's hands, since no one else would have me—if Grandfather had still lived.

At any rate, the peculiarities of my birth set aside, I certainly possessed no special gifts or abilities, nothing that would have caused such a strange spark to kindle between his lordship and myself. As I lay awake, staring up at the dimly lit ceiling in my chamber—for the fire had not yet gone out—I began to wonder if Lord Greymount had been asking the wrong question. Perhaps that spark had come from him, and had nothing to do with me.

Certainly, he did seem to be a strange man. Handsome, yes, but that quality only led me to ask why someone blessed with his appearance and wealth should be living in this grand castle with no wife, no children, only the bare necessities to ensure that the household ran more or less smoothly.

A household with no female servants. There was a knot I would dearly like to unravel, for I had certainly never heard of such a thing. Men were usually not the sorts to keep the scullery clean, or to scrub the chamber pots.

Unfortunately, it did not seem as if I would have answers to my questions any time in the near future. No, probably the best I could hope for now was that his lordship would let me alone, and suffer my presence in his castle until the storm abated at last and he sent me on my way.

That thought sent a pang through me, although I wasn't quite sure why.

After all, what difference did it make to me whether I ever saw Phelan Greymount again?

❧ Chapter Five ❧

Because my last meeting with Lord Greymount had been so disastrous, I truly thought I would be kept in my chamber for the duration of my stay in the castle. How long that might be, I did not know; when I awoke that next morning, the wind still howled and the snow still blew. Now I was quite sure that the drifts had covered the ground-floor windows. Perhaps it was more protected in the courtyard, where Master Merryk took those two beautiful dogs to get their exercise, but my room looked out over the open lands which led to the castle walls. In the summer, it was most likely a pleasant prospect, if those rolling hills were covered in green grass. Now, though, the landscape beyond my window was bleak and almost featureless, every landmark smoothed away by the enormous snow drifts.

When a knock came at my door, I was not terribly surprised. True, my morning meal had come and gone, but the steward did check in on me occasionally for reasons that had nothing to do with meals. I still had no entertainment, although by that point I had almost grown used to my idle state. Almost. Who would have ever thought that I would yearn for a pair of socks to darn?

I got up to open the door, then stood there, astonished. For the man standing before me was not Master Merryk, but Lord Greymount himself, with the dogs Doxen and Linsi nosing about in the corridor behind him.

"Good morning," he said pleasantly, as if that terrible scene between us had never occurred. "How are you today, Mistress Sendris?"

I bobbed probably the most inelegant curtsey he had ever seen, while at the same time a furious flush heated my cheeks. "I—I am quite well, your lordship."

"Excellent. Master Merryk tells me that my dogs have taken quite a liking to you. I thought it rather selfish to deprive them of your company."

Was that his oblique way of saying that he himself could have done very well without seeing me? I slanted a brief look up at him, but his expression was bland, betraying nothing. Whatever had caused his fury of the afternoon before, it seemed to have disappeared now. The sudden alteration in his behavior discomfited me, but I knew better than to let Phelan Greymount see how confused I was by his appearance at my door.

"They are very lovely dogs, my lord," I said, and that was true enough. "I should be glad to be better acquainted with them."

"Then call them to you," he told me, a slight curl at the corner of his mouth, as if he did not quite expect them to come at my command.

I was far from certain, either, but I told myself the worst that would happen was that they would ignore me, and perhaps Lord Greymount would have a chuckle at my expense. Well, I had suffered worse.

"Linsi, Doxen!" I called, leaning down slightly with my palms pressed against my skirts.

At once they left off smelling a particularly intriguing patch on the floor and trotted over, then sat down next to me. Both dogs looked up at once, clearly imploring me to scratch their ears again.

Which I did, even as I attempted to keep a smile of triumph from my lips.

"That is rather extraordinary," his lordship commented, watching the spectacle.

"How so? They seem like very friendly dogs."

"To you, perhaps." He crossed his arms. "But they are *fenskar*, dogs descended from the great white wolves of the north. They are fiercely loyal—but to one master only."

"They seem to tolerate Master Merryk well enough." I straightened so I could look up at him and not down at the dogs. They both whined gently, and Linsi appeared as if she wanted to scratch at my velvet skirts and then thought better of it.

"'Tolerate' being the relevant word here. They will go with him because I have trained them to obey his commands, but if any other member of the household should go near them without my permission—well, the outcome would not be pleasant."

I had a brief vision of the scarred man-at-arms having the seat of his trousers torn out by an angry Linsi, and had to fight to keep a smile from my lips. Of course I would never wish harm on another person, but a little embarrassment? That did not seem very terrible.

"So you see," Lord Greymount went on, "that is why I am rather astonished by their reaction to you. And since they must find it dull to be around me all the time, I thought it might be a treat for them to spend some time with you."

"Dull" was not usually a word I would associate with Phelan Greymount's company. Even now, though I was still rather off-balance from our last interaction, I couldn't prevent myself from taking in every detail of his appearance that I could—the way his sooty hair brushed against the collar of his doublet, the thin, finely cut lines of his mouth.

And that, I knew was foolish. I should not be admiring him. He was the lord of these lands, not some handsome apprentice I might find it amusing to flirt with. Not that Kerolton had all that many apprentices, handsome or otherwise.

"And you must find it tedious to be trapped in here, day after day. Let me show you something of the castle."

"I—I would like that, my lord," I said. At the same time, I hoped the tour he had planned would be confined to the upper levels. I had no great wish to see the scar-faced man-at-arms any time soon.

As if he would dare to act in such a way in his lord's presence, I scoffed at myself. *No, he would be on his very best behavior, I think.*

Most likely. Still, it never hurt to avoid a confrontation when possible.

"This way, then," Lord Greymount said, and headed off down the hallway.

I told myself I should be glad he had not offered me his arm, for I would not have known whether to accept it. At any rate, the dogs had decided to range back and forth between the two of us, sometimes close on his lordship's heels, and sometimes nearly stepping on the train of my dress, and it would have been difficult to walk arm in arm.

"The castle was built some three centuries ago," he told me with an absent wave of one arm. "By my great-great-—well, a great many 'greats' ago, I suppose. It has withstood fire and flood and siege, although I do find myself somewhat concerned by what this storm might wreak. Already the roof in one of the towers has given way under the weight of the snow."

"Oh, no!" I exclaimed, while at the same time finding myself glad that I had not been housed in one of those tower rooms.

A faint smile. "Oh, yes." But then he gave a negligent lift of his shoulders and said, "It is more a nuisance than anything else, as we were only using that tower for storage. However, we will still need to effect repairs at some point—if the storm ever lets up, that is."

"It must eventually."

Lord Greymount stopped then and turned toward me while wearing a smile that hovered somewhere between teasing and malicious. "Oh, eventually, I would suppose. But in my grandfather's time, there was a storm that lasted for thirty days and thirty nights, and they were reduced to eating the rats."

"The rats?" I could feel my eyes widening, even though I had the impression that he was telling a tall tale to force a reaction from me. "Why, I have seen no evidence of rats in Harrow Hall. It seems a very tidy place."

My reply only made his mouth twitch, even as the smile disappeared. "I will send your praise on to Master Merryk. No doubt he will be gratified that you find his housekeeping adequate. But I do not think we have much to fear. The castle is well-stocked, and although this storm is fierce enough, I misdoubt that it will range for another twenty-five days."

Which meant I'd already been trapped here for five days. I had thought the count lay somewhere in that vicinity, but truly, time already felt as if it had begun to run together, one day overlapping the next with no real distinction between them.

Five days. Everyone must think me dead by now. And how had my grandmother fared in this storm, out in her cottage all by herself? True, the supplies we had laid by would last twice as long, for she would only have to worry about feeding herself. Even so, they would run out eventually.

Something in Lord Greymount's expression shifted then. When he spoke, it was in a much gentler tone. "What is it, Mistress Sendris?"

"Oh," I said, and lifted a hand, as if to wave away my fears. "It is only that I was thinking of my grandmother, all alone in her cottage. She has no way of knowing that I am well, and while the cottage has a new roof and we had a good supply of food, it cannot last forever."

He shifted his weight from one foot to the other. Indeed, at first I thought he'd intended to step toward me, to perhaps offer some comfort. But no, that was a foolish notion. My sorrows must be of very little concern to him.

And if he had reached out to pat me on the arm, or made some other gesture, what on earth would I have done? The mere thought of him touching me again made a strange thrill go down my back.

Then he said, his voice a little too hearty, "I am sure she is faring much better than you fear. And I doubt very much that this storm will last the week. Soon enough we will be able to send word that you are well, even if it will not be safe for you to venture forth at that point."

"Why wouldn't it be?" I inquired. Linsi came up and pressed her cold nose against my fingers, and I gave her ears a scratch as I waited for Lord Greymount's reply.

"Have you ever walked through six-foot snow drifts, Mistress Sendris?"

"Not through them, no," I confessed. "But on top of them, yes. My grandfather had a pair of stout snowshoes, and he taught me how to use them when I was only a child. Do you not have such contrivances here at Harrow Hall?"

At those words, his lordship let out a laugh. Doxen, who'd settled himself at his feet while we paused to have our conversation, looked up, cocking his head to one side.

"Why, yes, we do, Mistress Sendris. After a storm such as this, it is the only way to get around, for even the horses are unable to venture forth. But I must confess that I would never have expected a young woman such as yourself to know how to use them."

"Well, perhaps when the storm subsides, we can snowshoe together, my lord."

He smiled—no, grinned—and shook his head. "Perhaps. In the meantime, let us press on."

As soon as we began to move, the dogs fell into place beside us. I thought how companionable that was, with Lord Greymount on my left and the dogs on either side, almost as if they knew something we didn't.

Again I wanted to shake my head at my overactive imagination. As he'd told me himself, he was only taking me on this expedition so the dogs might have some occupation beyond sleeping at his feet. To infer anything else from his behavior was quite ludicrous. All the same, it did feel quite grand to be walking at Phelan Greymount's side, almost as if we were equals, rather than master and supplicant.

We came to a door at the end of the hallway. I assumed the chamber which lay beyond that door was our destination, an assumption proved correct when he led me inside, saying, "Forgive me for not thinking of this earlier. It might have helped to pass the time for you."

I looked around and saw that I stood in a large room with a fine, tall window cut into the wall opposite the door. The view it afforded—which now was no more than the same blowing white I'd seen for the past five days—was probably not the reason why his lordship had brought me here, however. The other three walls were covered in shelves, and on those shelves sat a multitude of books. Tall books, short books, thin books, plump ones that practically begged to be held in your lap while you sat in bed.

Words quite failed me. I truly hadn't expected such riches to be concealed within the castle's walls, for although I had heard that an enterprising man in Sirlende had somehow invented a device that could print many books at once, rather than having a scribe labor over one for hours and hours, still they were costly things, worth almost their weight in gold.

Apparently discomfited by my awestruck silence, Lord Greymount sent me a piercing look. "Can you read?"

"Of course I can read!" I retorted, my tone sharper than I had intended.

"Forgive me, but that is not always a foregone conclusion with someone—" He paused then, as if realizing he'd been about to say something that might offend me.

The damage was done, however. I crossed my arms and tilted my chin up at him. "Someone of my station?"

"Well...yes."

Although I knew it was foolish for me to be vexed, I couldn't quite smother the flame of anger that burned somewhere deep in my breast. "I can read quite well, Lord Greymount," I said, not bothering to keep the irritation from my tone. "I must confess that I don't often have the leisure to do so, but—"

He held up a hand. "That will do, Mistress Sendris." A pause, during which he sent me a piercing look. "Do you mind if I ask you a question of a rather personal nature?"

That request sounded daunting. Nevertheless, I responded, as calmly as I could, "Not at all, my lord."

Even though I had granted him the permission to make the inquiry, he didn't speak at first, but rather went over to one of the bookshelves and ran a finger over the spines of the books that sat there. Doxen and Linsi gave him a questioning look, then seemed to decide he was not in the mood for ear scratching or other activities of interest to a dog, and lay down, their snouts almost touching. Despite my worry over what Lord Greymount was about to ask, I couldn't help smiling slightly.

Then his lordship turned back toward me. "I noted when we first spoke that you didn't sound much like a common villager, Mistress Sendris."

"Indeed? Then my grandmother would say her work was done."

His brows pulled together in obvious puzzlement at my response.

Relenting, I went on, "It is not that strange a story, my lord. My grandmother is not from Kerolton. Rather, she is the youngest daughter of a tin merchant from the mining town of Karthels, in the Ozar Hills."

"Then she is quite a long way from home, is she not?"

True enough. Karthels lay nearly thirty leagues from the village that had been my only home. I had never seen it, and when I tried to get my grandmother to tell me more of the town where she was born, she'd only shaken her head and said there was not much to tell, that mining towns were never known for their beauty and that she much preferred the forests of Sarisfell.

"Yes, your lordship, she is rather far from where she began," I replied. His expression was so neutral that I could not tell what he thought of my answer—whether it bored him, or whether he found it interesting that my heritage was slightly more elevated than he had thought. "But my grandfather traveled to Karthels one summer, to see the closest town of any real note, and there he met my grandmother."

"And your grandfather's vocation?"

"He was a hunter and trapper, my lord."

At this response, Lord Greymount raised an eyebrow. "I cannot think that a tin merchant would have been overly impressed by such credentials."

"Well, of course I was not there"—his lordship flashed me a quick grin at that disclaimer—"but to hear my grandmother tell it, my grandfather was quite a handsome man in his day. He told her of the beauties of the forest, so unlike the bare hillsides of Karthels, and wooed her away from her family. And so they came to Sarisfell, where she has lived ever since."

"How very romantic," said Lord Greymount, in tones which seemed to indicate that he thought precisely the opposite. Well, I supposed to one such as him, the love between a forest hunter and the youngest daughter of a tin merchant was no very great thing.

"She thought so," I said lightly. "At any rate, she was in charge of my education, and so she taught me how to speak like a young woman of good birth, to read and write and do my sums. It is more than most of the others in Kerolton have had, although she did try to teach some of the village children, back when my mother was a little girl. But the other villagers did not like that, thought she was putting on airs, and they told her their children had more worthy activities to occupy their time, and that was the end of the matter."

"I see." He frowned, as if turning the information I had provided over in his mind. "You do not speak much of your mother. That is, you did not say anything to me about whether or not she is worried by your absence."

"That would be difficult, my lord, seeing as she is dead." At least, that was the story I always told myself. She would not be so very old, barely four decades, and so I supposed she could be alive somewhere. But I did not want to think that she yet lived and had never returned to see how I fared. It was easier to believe her dead.

His response was swift. "I am sorry."

"Thank you, but she has been gone since I was very young. I barely remember her." Which was true enough. Something about a pair of shining blue eyes, and wavy deep brown hair that fell to her waist, hair that flew out all around her as she lifted me into the air and twirled me around and around. That was my clearest memory of her, of the way the sun had slanted down into the clearing where we stood and awakened glints of copper and bronze in her dark hair. She had been so very beautiful. No wonder Amery Willar had wanted to make her his wife, even though she'd disgraced herself by bringing a bastard child into the world.

Somehow I knew what Lord Greymount was going to say next. I could feel myself stiffen as the words left his mouth.

"And your father?"

I knew it was silly to worry about what Phelan Greymount might think of me. Even so, I found myself hesitating, attempting to think of the best way to answer his question without condemning myself forever in his eyes. In that moment, I hated how the world had assigned guilt to me for something that had been none of my doing. I certainly had not asked to be born.

But then I pulled in a breath and made myself face him squarely. Perhaps he would see that as an impertinence, that I would look up into his eyes with all the boldness of an equal, but I would not quail before him, not when I was about to tell him how truly mean my birth had been.

"I do not know, my lord."

My answer surprised him, that I could tell. His eyes widened, and I saw shock register there before his expression smoothed itself back to its usual impassivity. "Your mother never spoke of him?"

"Not that I know of. She was...gone...before I was old enough to ask for any real details. But my grandmother vows that my mother never confided in her, either."

"That is quite...extraordinary."

That's one word for it, I thought with some bitterness. All I could do, though, was lift my shoulders, willing him to take my apparent indifference at face value, and to not look too closely in my eyes, so he might glimpse the hurt that still lurked there, even after so many years.

"You do not see it that way," he said then, and again I was surprised by the gentleness in his voice.

"How could I? To be viewed as one worthy of scorn, to be called 'fatherless' and 'bastard' and far, far worse? My grandmother did what she could to shield me, but children can be cruel, especially to anyone they see as different from themselves."

His mouth tightened, and for a moment he said nothing. As if sensing my distress, Linsi got up from where she lay on the floor and came over to me, then leaned her beautiful white head against my knee. For some reason, the sweet, simple gesture made tears sting at my eyes, but I blinked them away, instead concentrating on running my fingers through her soft fur so I might let that small comfort soothe my soul.

Lord Greymount did not miss any of that; his gaze flicked down to the dog, and then up to my face. "But you see," he said, "in a way, is that not freeing? Your father could have been anyone, from a great lord to a traveling tinker. You are able to invent him as anything you like, because you do not have the weight of history and heritage to tie you down."

I wondered what heritage he fought against, for although his tone was even enough, I thought I could detect a trace of bitterness at the edges of his voice. "That is a pretty way of looking at the situation," I replied. "Would that I had thought of it when the village children were teasing me."

And doing far worse than merely addressing me by whatever cruel epithets they could think of. I certainly would not speak of such things to Phelan Greymount, but when I grew older, and took on some of my mother's beauty, there were young men in the village who thought because she had been loose with her virtues, then her daughter should behave the same way. I learned to be fleet of foot, and to do whatever I could not to be caught alone.

Despite those precautions, there had been one notable instance soon after I turned sixteen, when I'd had to club Ilan Martis over the head with a heavy tree branch so I could flee before anything more terrible happened. I'd never spoken of the incident to my grandmother, for I knew she would have taken up the matter with Ilan's father. As for Ilan himself, well, he was mortified enough that a girl had gotten the better of him that he'd never mentioned it again. Ever after, he'd sent me angry, sidelong looks when I came to the village, but I shrugged off his smoldering resentment. The important thing was that he'd given me a wide berth afterward, apparently wishing to find easier prey. He had married the year after, to one of the miller's numerous daughters, and that had been the end of the affair.

"I am sorry for that," Lord Greymount said, and I shot him a look of surprise.

"Why should you be sorry, my lord? You were not the one taunting me."

"I suppose it is only that it troubles me to think of a lovely young woman having to endure such torments."

I was not sure how best to respond to such a statement, for hearing him call me lovely quite put me off balance. He had hinted at such compliments previously, but had never been so bald-faced about his admiration. In that moment, I decided it was best to pretend he had not mentioned my appearance at all. "I thank you for your concern, but that was years ago. We have all grown up, and those who were my tormentors are too busy with their own families to trouble themselves with me."

"But you have no family of your own."

It was not a question. I did not quite sigh, but I did expel a small breath, then gave Linsi a final pat on her head before I straightened and met Lord Greymount's curious dark gaze. "No. Most of those in the village were not interested in aligning themselves with a fatherless young woman."

"Most...but not all?"

I had already told his lordship most of my secrets, so it did not seem to me that it mattered whether I relinquished one more. "Clem Wisegrot, one of the wealthiest men in Kerolton, did ask for my hand, but I refused him."

This revelation elicited another lift of Lord Greymount's strong brows. "Indeed? I take it his wealth was not enough to recommend him?"

"No, and neither was the idea of playing nursemaid to his late wife's three children."

A chuckle. "You are not fond of children, Mistress Sendris?"

"I am very fond of children," I said calmly. "What I am not particularly fond of is wild beasts masquerading as children."

This time his lordship's response was an outright laugh, and another of those flashing grins, the ones that sent a strange tingling warmth straight to the depths of my belly. "No, I can't imagine most people would be fond of such children. It seems you made a wise choice."

"Most people in the village did not think so. They thought it was simply more evidence of my strange and fey nature, for any young woman with a bit of common sense should have jumped at such an advantageous match, wild brood of children or no."

"Is your nature truly so strange? You seem to me to be a young woman of rare common sense."

His praise only warmed me that much more, but I made myself shrug. "Perhaps you simply have not had the acquaintance of many young women. I cannot help but notice that you have none working for you here at Harrow Hall."

That remark did not appear to sit well with him; he did not exactly stiffen, but I detected a brief tightening of his mouth before he said, "A choice made for a number of reasons. You did have the misfortune to make the acquaintance of several of my men-at-arms, after all. A young serving woman would have to be always on her guard around such men."

"I am sure they would learn to behave themselves, if you but spoke a word on the subject. And if they did not behave, could you not dismiss them?"

"More common sense, Mistress Sendris?" This time the smile he sent me was somewhat strained, and never reached his eyes. "My answer is that they are very good at what they do, and up here at the very northern reaches of our land, it is more important for me to have experienced men-at-arms who can defend this place if necessary, rather than to have women working in my household."

I wanted to ask why Harrow Hall was in such need of defense, when the land had been at peace—at least, as far as I knew—for almost as long as I'd been alive. Yes, there was the occasional skirmish along the border North Eredor shared with Sirlende, but those small clashes took place off to the west, very far from here.

"I see, my lord," I said, although I didn't. Not really. But I was beginning to learn enough of Phelan Greymount's humors that I could tell when it was better not to ask any more questions.

A nod, and then he said, "But perhaps you should choose?"

"'Choose'?" I repeated, rather stupidly, for I couldn't guess what he might be referring to.

He waved his hand toward the crowded bookshelves. "Something to occupy your time while we wait out this storm. That was the reason I brought you here, after all."

Of course. Our conversation had so occupied me that I'd quite forgotten his comment about my taking some books to read. I summoned a smile, saying, "Oh, that is correct. Shall I take two or three, and then perhaps come to fetch more if the storm should prove to last longer than it will take me to read them?"

"Take as many as you can carry," he told me. "For it would be easier if you did not have to make frequent trips here to replace the ones you have already read."

His unspoken meaning was clear—or at least it seemed clear enough to me. I should not expect him to be the one to help me while away the hours. This small excursion, or whatever I wished to call it, would not necessarily be repeated.

Well, at least not until he or the dogs grew dull once again, and needed some novelty to break up their days.

I nodded and murmured, "of course," and went over to the nearest set of shelves. A good deal of what I saw there was on practical topics, such as hunting and fishing and the raising of dogs, but there were also histories of North Eredor and its neighbors, and books of maps and geography. I selected as many of these as I could, stacking five of them in my arms before I realized that one more on the pile would probably cause the entire thing to topple.

"Let me help you with those," Lord Greymount offered, scooping them up as they began to lean dangerously to one side. I noticed that he was careful not to touch me, however, just as he had avoided offering me his arm earlier. So whatever that strange spark was that had leapt between us, he did not wish to have it happen again.

I knew I could not ask him about that, however. Instead, I protested, "Oh, no, they're fine—"

"They were most decidedly not fine," he said. "Another moment, and at least the top two or three would have been on the floor."

I bit back another objection, for clearly he did not intend to allow me to carry the books myself. While I appreciated the chivalry of the gesture, I could not help but be somewhat dismayed at the sight of the lord of the manor carrying those books for me.

"Oh, Mistress Sendris," he said with a chuckle, "please remove that look of distress from your face. I do not mind at all being your beast of burden."

The dancing light in his eyes was infectious, and a welcome relief from his sober expression earlier, when I worried that I had offended him. I offered him a smile, and said, "I suppose better you than Linsi or Doxen. I have a feeling that neither of them would take very kindly to being asked to carry those books back to my chamber."

"No, they most decidedly would not. I know this in truth, for when I was a boy and had their grandfather as my companion, I tried to get him to carry several of my toys on his back so that I might have him take them out to the courtyard. Let us just say that the toys were flung everywhere with great abandon, and Rix did not forgive me for several days."

I tried to imagine Phelan Greymount as a young boy, but had some difficulty. He was so tall and strong that I could not picture him in my mind's eye as anything other than how I saw him now.

Since he had made no mention of any siblings, I thought I knew the answer already, but I felt compelled to ask anyway. "Were you an only child?"

He shifted the books he carried, and gave a slight lift of his shoulders. "Yes. That is, I should have had a younger brother, but my mother died while attempting to give birth to him, and he died as well."

I wished I had not asked, because the light had quite gone from his eyes as he made that reply. "I am so very sorry."

"You need not trouble yourself. I was not yet three years old when my mother passed away, and, like you and your own mother, I can barely remember her. My father remarried, but she died in childbirth as well, and I suppose at that point he decided he had had enough of burying wives."

Nothing I could think to say felt right, so I only nodded. It was not that uncommon a story, unfortunately; we women always took a risk when bringing new life into the world. My fingers brushed against the wool of my skirts, and I recalled that the gowns hanging in the wardrobe, and which I had been borrowing, had belonged to her. Did Lord Greymount think it odd to see me in them? But no, he had lost his mother very early on, and did not remember much of her. I somehow doubted that the few memories he had left had anything to do with what she had worn.

It seemed that he had had enough of conversation, for he began to move toward the door, his arms still full of books. Linsi and Doxen immediately leapt up and ran out into the hallway, clearly glad for this chance at some more exercise. I followed, feeling oddly tongue-tied. We had shared some confidences, his lordship and I, and yet it was all too obvious that he was the one to set the rules for what would be spoken of and what would not. It was clear enough to me that he had had sufficient conversation on the topic of his family.

Whether he regretted anything of what he'd said to me, I could not know. For myself, I felt almost a sensation of relief. I had told him the worst, and yet the revelations about my parentage had not made him recoil in disgust, or treat me with any condescension. He could be high-handed, true, but I thought that aspect of his character had rather more to do with the station he'd been born to rather than his true nature.

We returned to my chamber, and he insisted on going inside so he could set the books down on one of the side tables there. I had always thought the room quite grand in scale, for it seemed to dwarf me when I was alone in it, but now it appeared almost filled now that it had Lord Greymount contained within its walls. And also, I couldn't help feeling a certain rush of blood heat my cheeks as I looked past him to the bed, although he paid the furnishings no mind.

"There," he said, giving the topmost book on the pile a tap with one finger before he turned back toward me. "That should occupy you for some time, Mistress Sendris."

"Thank you for bringing them here," I replied. "And for allowing me to take them from your library."

"You are welcome." He paused for a moment, and it seemed that his gaze lingered on my mouth.

Oh, gods. Could it be that he intended to kiss me? Yes, he'd avoided touching me during the entire time we'd been together, but....

We were all alone here. Perhaps it had been foolish to allow him inside my chamber. Perhaps he had begun to think as the young men of Kerolton had, that a woman whose mother possessed an easy virtue might very well share her same weaknesses.

My heart began to beat a little faster, and I wondered then what I would do if he did bend down and lay his lips against mine. The proper response, of course, would be to back away and act offended that he would take such a liberty.

Right then, however, I wasn't sure whether I would mind terribly if he did take that liberty.

But then he gave me a small bow and said, "Happy reading, Mistress Sendris. It is time to take the dogs down for their exercise, but I am sure they enjoyed sharing your company this afternoon. Have a pleasant evening."

And with those words, he went out and shut the door behind him, and I was left quite alone.

Chapter Six

Although I was glad of the books Lord Greymount had so graciously brought to my room for me, I did not immediately pick one up. Instead, I went to the window and gazed out at the ever-falling snow, and pondered all that had passed between us. It would be foolish to deny I had begun to feel some sort of attraction to him, so I did not bother to do so. I did, however, scold myself for allowing that weakness to creep into my spirit. My heart was ever barricaded behind a high wall. It had seemed the safest course for me, for I doubted any man I wanted was someone who would want me in return. No, my only value lay in being someone's nursemaid, as Clem Wisegrot had made all too clear. Certainly no one else had ever offered for me, or showed any interest, save the sort I did not desire in the least. I had done my best to ignore the strange, lonely ache I felt in my heart as I lay down to sleep in my grandmother's cottage, telling myself that an empty bed was better than one occupied by a man I did not love.

Now, though...I had spent an hour in Phelan Greymount's company, and even though he was gone, it seemed as if he somehow lingered in my chamber, his presence still filling the room. I could hear his voice, could see the glint in his dark eyes as he teased me. Did he have any idea as to his effect on me, or was he oblivious? He'd shown no sign, but that did not mean much. I was not at all acquainted with men of his station, and so I had very little idea as to how they might act around a young woman, even one who was far beneath them in status.

I leaned my head against the draperies, feeling the soft nap of the velvet beneath my cheek. It did not comfort me, however. In that moment, I found myself missing my grandmother with a fierce, strange ache. Yes, I was a grown woman and well able to manage my own affairs, but she could have offered some advice, or at least told me it was of no use to berate myself for falling under the spell of a man who was so utterly unlike anyone else I had ever met.

It would have been better if he had not looked at me like that, there at the end. Perhaps I flattered myself, but I had seen desire in men's eyes before, and I was almost certain that was what I had glimpsed in Lord Greymount's expression before he turned away from me and professed his concern over getting his dogs down to their exercise on time. He could have sensed that desire and told himself I was his guest, and so he could not take such an advantage.

Or perhaps he had simply realized I was so far beneath him that he should not sully himself by kissing me.

Biting back a sigh, I turned from the window and went to the stack of books, which looked as if they might overwhelm the spindly little carved table where they sat. The one on top was a work of geography, complete with carefully hand-drawn maps, the countries and oceans and rivers all called out in equally neat lettering.

I was surprised to see how much open country there was beyond Harrow Hall, how North Eredor's borders extended all the way up to the Great Ice Sea. There were no other towns or villages that I could see on that map, and so it seemed Lord Greymount's claim that his was the last bulwark against the wild lands was true.

What was out there, really? Only miles and miles of wild wastelands? I had heard tales of giants that roamed the frozen wastes, and fey, evil spirits that haunted those frozen, empty places, but I had always thought they were only that—tales, and nothing more. Perhaps Harrow Hall was more than a lonely castle, and instead my land's last defense against those enemies that lurked in the dark and the cold.

Outside the window, the wind howled, gaining in strength, and I shivered. It would be all too easy to believe those eerie sounds emanated from some fell creature, and not merely from a high wind weaving amongst the towers of the castle.

Suddenly, geography did not seem quite as comforting as I'd thought it would be.

I put the book aside and selected another. A history of North Eredor should do very well. I did not know all that much on the subject, save that once Eredor has been a single great land, before the mage wars tore it asunder nearly a thousand years ago. Much had been lost in those wars, knowledge that could never be regained...but perhaps it was better that way. Knowledge of terrible power was what caused those wars, and after they were done, magic disappeared from all the lands of the continent, its practitioners hunted down and destroyed so they might not spread their evil anymore.

The book I had chosen was quite dry and factual, and made no mention of giants or spirits or anything more deadly than the *corraghar*, the ancient hill tribes who called themselves the people of the wolf. I had never seen one of the *corraghar*, for the lands they called their own lay mainly to the south and east of the forest of Sarisfell where I had lived my entire life, but I knew they were fierce fighters, dark and strange, and kept to themselves, not mixing much with the rest of North Eredor's population. Indeed, the lord of our land, Kadar Arkalis, was half *corraghar*, although it did not seem to me that his mixed blood had done much to bring the corraghar in contact with those who also called the North home.

Still, it was interesting to note that the contested lands on the western marches had always been part of Eredor even before it was split north and south, and it was only because Sirlende had expanded and expanded, gobbling up small principalities on its marches to become the greatest empire on the continent, that it set its eyes on those lands that comprised the northwest edge of North Eredor's borders. But the Eredorians would not give up, and so neither side ever gained true supremacy there, since it seemed the Sirlendian emperors did not think those hardscrabble lands worth an all-out war.

I thought it must be rather hard for the people who lived in the disputed region, and counted myself lucky that I had grown up in Sarisfell, which was several hundred leagues from the western border of my land. We certainly did not have to worry about invading Sirlendians—or marauding *corraghar*—but instead enjoyed sheltered lives for the most part.

The light began to fail as I read, so I put the book aside and went to light some more candles in addition to the one on the dressing table, which I'd kept burning because of the day's general gloom. As I was finishing this task, a knock came at the door. My heart lifted, and I hurried to answer the knock, hoping that Lord Greymount would be waiting outside.

Alas, it was only the steward with the tray that held my evening meal.

I forced a smile to my lips, even as I stepped aside so he could enter the room. "Thank you, Master Merryk."

He offered a smile in return, but something about it appeared rather stiff, as if he only smiled because he knew he must. Because the table where he usually placed the tray was now piled high with books, he had to go over to the dressing table and set my meal down there. "It seems you now have quite enough to keep you occupied, Mistress Sendris."

"Ah, yes," I replied, knowing that a blush spread over my cheeks as I spoke. I could only hope the room wasn't so brightly lit that he would notice. "His lordship was very generous with his library. I have rather an embarrassment of riches now."

"So you do." He paused for a moment, then said, "You were exploring for a good while, it seems."

"An hour or so, yes." Did the steward disapprove of his master spending time in my company? I supposed that wasn't outside the bounds of possibility, although Master Merryk had always seemed to be very kind to me. Or was he only kind when he thought there was no chance of a dalliance between Lord Greymount and myself?

And there is still no chance, I told myself. *A bit of time spent in company with someone, and a glance that could have been entirely misinterpreted, is not quite enough reason for you to have any kind of expectations.*

"His dogs are very lovely," I added, hoping that would be a more neutral topic. After all, his lordship had claimed the dogs as one of the chief reasons for coming to get me and show me something of the castle, although in truth, the tour had stopped short as soon as we reached the library. Did that mean Lord Greymount intended to show me more as time went on?

Something about Master Merryk's expression seemed to relax slightly. "Yes, they are, although they are getting as restless as all of us, cooped up day after day while the storm does its work."

"And there still is no sign of it stopping?"

"None that any of us have been able to tell, even those who are stationed in the towers to keep watch. Not one break since it began. It is very strange."

So it was. I had certainly never experienced another storm of such ferocity and duration. It was almost enough to make one believe that some kind of evil force did lurk out in the wastelands beyond Harrow Hall, and had sent the snow and the wind and the cold out of some spiteful delight in seeing others suffer.

Not that we were suffering all that terribly, at least not yet. I had not seen any kind of worry about the castle's supplies, whether of firewood or foodstuffs, and so I supposed they had

had a great deal laid in against the coming of winter. But the castle's inhabitants had to be consuming food and wood at a far greater rate than originally planned. What if this storm went on and on, and gave no opportunity to replenish those stores?

Now you are just being foolish. All storms must come to an end eventually. So will this one, and then Lord Greymount's men will be able to go out to hunt and gather firewood.

And escort me home, most likely. A little pang went through me at that thought. As much as I did not like being cooped up in this castle for days on end—for I was used to going out into the woods to gather herbs and leaves and bark for my dyes, even in harsh weather—I liked rather less the thought of never seeing Phelan Greymount again.

My tone perhaps too hearty, I said, "Well, let us hope that we will all awake to a morning of bright sunshine, Master Merryk. Stranger things have happened."

He nodded, then took his leave of me and let himself out. I went to the dressing table and sat down, knowing I must eat quickly before everything grew cold. Once again, the meal was quite fine—roasted chicken and potatoes, an apple, a cup of warm cider. More than I would have gotten at home, most likely, where we would have been keeping a careful watch on what we consumed so as not to run out.

I wondered where the castle's chicken coop was located. Out in the courtyard somewhere seemed the most logical placement, but I knew that, even protected by a coop, chickens would never be able to survive such a ferocious storm. Had the animals been brought inside so they might be housed safely within the castle's walls?

That question brought an image of the scar-faced man-at-arms and his compatriots having to dodge a flock of cranky chickens wandering around their quarters, and I smiled, then took a healthy swallow of the warm spiced cider Master Merryk had provided. That cider did help to improve my mood, and I told myself that worrying would certainly not change anything, except possibly to keep me from sleeping as well as I might.

But perhaps it was because I had gotten rather more exercise that day than I normally did...or because after I had gotten myself ready to sleep, I took the history book with me into bed, thinking I would read a few more pages before I slipped into slumber...I did slide away into oblivion without even noticing, darkness enveloping me as my head fell against the pillows and the book dropped down onto the covers.

I had not dreamt much since coming to Harrow Hall, or at least, I did not recall anything of what I dreamed. That night, though, almost as soon as I shut my eyes, I found myself standing on a great white expanse, snow stretching pure and untouched in every direction, as if I had been dropped there rather than walking to reach my current position. I could see no sun overhead, but neither was the day cloudy. Instead, the sky was a vast expanse of smooth, uniform grey, as featureless as the snowy landscape on which I stood.

A great cloak of white fur covered me to my chin, and I felt nothing of the cold, although a brisk wind blew, pulling my hair free from the knot at the back of my head and whipping the loose strands around my face. I began to move forward, and realized I had a pair of snowshoes strapped to my feet, allowing me to move smoothly across the snowy ground. In my dream,

I smiled, happy to be moving forward, even though I truly did not know where I was going. After all, I could see nothing around me, only what seemed to be miles of open land.

Out of the corner of my eye, however, I thought I glimpsed several dark shapes. I stopped and looked back over my shoulder, and the breath caught in my throat. They were moving swiftly, galloping over the snow as if it did not slow them down at all. As they came closer, I realized the shapes were three great grey wolves, all apparently intent on running me down.

At once I began to surge forward as quickly as I could. One of the snowshoes caught the edge of my heavy, dragging cloak, and impatiently I threw off the garment, even though in real life I would never have done something so foolish. Underneath the cloak, I wore the blue and silver gown that hung in my wardrobe, the one I had not yet been brave enough to wear in real life. Now it flowed behind me, its hem becoming increasingly heavy with snow and wet.

Although my dream-self moved far more swiftly than I would have been able to manage in the waking world, still the gap between the wolves and me closed with frightening speed. Eyes watering with fear, I kept going, and wouldn't allow myself to look back yet another time, for doing so would only slow me down.

My hoarse breaths sounded loud as thunder. I pushed forward, knowing that to do anything else would end in certain death. But still the wolves grew closer. Now I could hear them panting, hear their padding footfalls against the powdery surface of the snow.

And then they were there, catching the hem of my dress in their teeth, so that I stumbled and fell face first into the snow. I pulled myself along, bare fingers digging into the icy surface, feeling it burn as it touched my exposed skin. But they were on me, snarling. One of them took the fur collar of my gown in its fangs and jerked, forcing me to roll over on my back.

I lay there, staring up into its golden eyes. It stared back at me, pink tongue lolling from its mouth. I wanted to shut my own eyes, since I knew what was about to come next, and yet somehow I couldn't. They remained wide open, making it seem as if I was slowly falling into the wolf's baleful golden glare.

Don't, I thought in my dream. *Please.*

For the longest moment, we both remained like that, frozen in place. The other two wolves had gone very still, and sat off to one side, watching us. And then the wolf lunged, and I screamed, screams that tore my throat even as his teeth sank into my neck, drawing out my life blood—

Those screams seemed to bounce off the walls of my room. I sat up in bed, blinking at my surroundings. One hand touched the leather binding of the book I had dropped, and I let out a small whimper. I was safe. Yes, the wind still howled outside quite as fiercely as those dream-wolves had, but I knew I had nothing to fear from it. Nothing could hurt me in here.

No one came to see what I had been screaming about. I reflected that I seemed to be the only person occupying a room on this floor, and so there was no one around who could have possibly heard my cries. Just as well; I wouldn't have liked to explain why a dream had affected me so badly that I'd awoken screaming as if someone had attacked me in my bed.

Which, I realized then, wasn't entirely outside the bounds of possibility. Yes, I locked the door behind me each night, but locks weren't infallible. What if the scar-faced man-at-arms got it into his head to come creeping up here one night, to take advantage of my isolation and force himself on me?

No, that would never happen. Surely no man would risk his position in Lord Greymount's guard for a few stolen moments with a woman. But then I remembered the way the man-at-arms had leered at me, and fingers of ice dragged their way down my back.

Wincing at the cold, I pushed the covers off and went to the door, then tested the lock. It was made of black iron, and seemed quite sturdy. Even so, I could not find myself terribly reassured. Perhaps it was only the dregs of the nightmare lingering in my mind, but I felt that lock was not nearly protection enough.

Glancing around, I noted the chair at the dressing table. It was carved from dark oak, and seemed to be the best solution. I went and fetched it, then shoved it up under the door handle. It might not hold if enough force was brought to bear, but at the very least it would make quite the racket when pushed out of the way, and that should be enough to warn me. Then I might have time to run to the hearth and snatch up the fireplace poker. Or perhaps I should bring the poker to the bed with me. No, that would require far too many explanations, if I should be caught that way.

Speaking of which, the fire had guttered out to almost nothing. No wonder the room was so cold. I'd quite forgotten to bank it down before climbing into bed, and I chided myself for my absent-mindedness.

I had no dressing gown, so I pulled the coverlet from the bed and wrapped it around myself before going to the hearth and plucking several logs from the basket which sat next to it. My supply was getting rather low, but I knew that it would be replenished in the morning, and I should be able to make do with what was here now.

The embers were still warm, and flared into life when I prodded them with the fireplace poker. Once I'd set the fresh logs on the grate, they caught soon enough, sending a welcome wave of warmth into the room. Would it be enough, though? What if the cold kept increasing until even a fire was not sufficient to keep away the bitter chill?

And what if those giants of legend came storming down from the north and battered down the castle's gates with their great clubs? I asked myself with some scorn. *I daresay that is equally as likely. In the meantime, you should calm yourself and go back to bed. One nightmare is not enough to completely shatter your common sense, is it?*

Perhaps not. Yet it was such a terrible dream...and so very real. In most cases, when I dreamed, I remembered very little of what had passed through my mind. Or if I did recall what I had been dreaming, it made little sense, people coming and going in no logical order, saying things that sounded nonsensical upon closer inspection. But in this instance, the events of my dream made all too much sense. Getting attacked by wolves was not such an out of the ordinary occurrence, although we rarely saw those predators in the forest of Sarisfell; it was too well hunted, and the wolves preferred to go someplace where they were the hunters, not the prey. It was only because our goat Sissi had broken out of her pen that she'd been caught, and slaughtered. If she had stayed close to the cottage, she would have been safe.

I shook my head at myself, then went back to the bed and slipped under the sheets and blankets, settling the coverlet over all the other layers. Already I could feel the room growing warmer, but somewhere deep within me was a core of ice that didn't want to thaw.

And when I closed my eyes, I felt the bite of the wolf's jaws once again.

Chapter Seven

I awoke to a pounding on the door and Master Merryk's voice calling, "Mistress Sendris? Is everything well with you?"

Opening a bleary eye, I required a moment or two to gather my wits. Falling asleep again had been difficult, but somewhere in the depths of the night, I had finally succumbed, dropping into a black, dreamless slumber. Because I had been so restless before that, I must have slept far later than usual.

The reason for the steward's consternation became clear enough as I focused on the door and saw that the chair I had placed there the night before was still firmly lodged under the handle. No wonder he was upset, for he must have tried the handle and realized the door was blocked somehow.

"One moment!" I scrambled out of bed, pulling the coverlet around me once more. I hurried over and removed the chair, then opened the door. "I am so very sorry."

Master Merryk stared down at me, iron-grey brows knitted together, his blue-grey eyes both worried and puzzled. "Did something happen last night?" he asked.

"N-no," I managed, stepping out of the way so he might go to the dressing table and set the tray he carried down upon its surface. "That is—oh, it sounds foolish now, but I had a very terrible dream, and when I awoke, I did not feel quite—quite safe. So I put the chair there. I did sleep very well after that, but I am sorry if it gave you a start."

He did not answer at first, but went and fetched the chair and put it in its proper place in front of the table. When he turned around, his frown had not yet gone. "Do you not feel safe here, Mistress Sendris?"

What a question! If he had asked me such a thing even a day earlier, I might not have hesitated. But my dream had not faded, was somehow as strong now in the cold, grey light of a snowy morning as it had been in the depths of the black night before. Which I knew was foolish. Dreams were not real, and no wolf could harm me here in this mighty castle, with its high walls and gates of steel.

"Of course I feel safe," I said stoutly, even as I held a private reservation in my heart. "You have all taken very good care of me. It is only that I felt so very unsettled after experiencing that dream, and I suppose I was still half asleep and not thinking clearly."

In that moment, his eyes appeared far too keen, too searching. "And what was this dream which terrified you so, Mistress Sendris?"

"Oh," I began, then waved a dismissive hand. Something within me was whispering not to tell him of what I had seen in that dream, and so I went on, tone too light, "You know how it is with dreams. They can seem so real, and so terrifying, at the time, and yet when you awake, they are gone as quickly as mist dissolving in sunlight. I cannot say—something about running, being pursued, but I don't remember anything more than that."

"Well, those sorts of dreams can be frightening, to be sure," the steward said. His gaze flicked toward the rumpled bed, and where the history book still lay discarded within the folds of the blankets. "Perhaps it is better not to be reading such things immediately before you go to sleep."

"I suppose you are right about that. Next time I will try something rather more innocuous —a book of herb lore, perhaps."

"A very good idea." He went to move toward the door, then paused. "Enjoy your breakfast, Mistress Sendris."

"Thank you, Master Merryk. I will."

He left and shut the door. I stood in the middle of the chamber, irresolute, then strode to the doorway and turned the lock. It was possible that he heard it, or perhaps he was already far enough away that he would not be able to detect the slight *click* as the tumblers fell into place.

But as I went back toward the table and my neglected breakfast, my eyebrows pulled together in their own frown. Always before Master Merryk had knocked at the door and waited for me to open it, but it seemed clear enough to me that today he had tried lifting the handle and found it locked, and only then began calling out to me. Had he knocked before that? I supposed it was possible I had been so deeply asleep that I hadn't heard him, although such behavior was very unlike me.

Still, I couldn't help but be disturbed that he would attempt to come in while I was still asleep. There could be a perfectly reasonable explanation for his behavior, although I did not know if I would have the courage to ask him why he had attempted to enter my room without my permission.

I glanced at the door one last time, then told myself it was daytime and the entire castle awake by now. Whatever Master Merryk's motivations, I should be perfectly safe now.

So I sat down and attended to my morning meal, which was not quite as lavish as the previous ones, consisting as it did of porridge and dried currants, and a small pot of tea. But at least it was warm and filling, and made me a little more sanguine about facing the day ahead.

After I had washed my face and brushed my hair, and attended to other needs before putting on another of those lovely borrowed dresses, I could not help experiencing a pang at the thought of yet another empty day stretching ahead of me. Some might have said that I should be used to my confinement after nearly a week of it, but my small expedition with Lord Greymount had left me craving his company, certain that nothing else but the sound of his voice, the sight of his face, could possibly serve to occupy my time.

Which I knew was unreasonable, and silly. I had no doubt that his lordship had many things to do, all of which were probably far more important than entertaining his unexpected and unwelcome guest. He had provided books for me to read, and that would have to be enough to fill the hours.

But still....

Once again I went to the window and looked outside. What I had expected to see, I did not know, for yet again there were those interminable veils of white, moving in their own lovely and mysterious patterns. The snow was beautiful, true, but its force had begun to frighten me, and not for myself any longer. I was, as I had told Master Merryk, quite safe here in this fortress of stone and steel. But what of my grandmother, in our small cottage with its walls of daub and thatched roof? Yes, we had replaced that roof recently, but even a new roof might not be able to hold up under the weight of so much snow.

I had to close my eyes against a sudden vision of that roof collapsed, and my grandmother buried beneath it. But no, I would not allow myself to believe she had suffered such a calamity. My grandmother was a wise woman, and if the cottage had begun to show signs of weakening, she would have taken the cat and gone into Kerolton, where I knew Amery Willar would have offered her shelter. His house was made of stone, and had a stout roof of tin. I had no doubt it would be able to withstand even a storm such as this.

Besides, the forest itself would have offered some shelter, the trees providing something of a barrier to the relentless wind and driving snow. Kerolton would enjoy far more protection than Harrow Hall, which stood on the edge of a moor, where the winds could come howling directly from the north with no trees or any other structures to provide some protection. Yes, its position offered a commanding view of the countryside around it—or at least it would in clear weather—but sheltered it most definitely was not.

I went to the stack of books on the little side table where I had left them and began studying their spines. More histories, and one on the trees and plants of North Eredor. Those I felt intimately acquainted with, since I had spent so much time studying their various components, and how they might be used to tint wool brown, or green, or even orange or grey or dull red. Still, it seemed a safer choice, judging by my reaction to reading the geography and history books the night before.

After tending the fire, and using up the last of my firewood—I had to hope someone would be by with a fresh bundle—I settled myself down in the chair and picked up the book I had selected. The drawings it contained were quite lovely, intricate and detailed, and yet I found my attention wandering.

Would the lack of firewood be enough of an excuse to send me out into the castle in search of some more? I had not fared so well when I'd ventured forth alone before, but at least now I knew something of what to expect. It would not be so very difficult to avoid the main hall altogether, but instead stay to the upper floors, in the hope that I might encounter Master Merryk and ask for more firewood.

Oh, do not fool yourself, I thought then. *If you went wandering those corridors, it is not Master Merryk you would wish to meet.*

Very well, that was true enough. I had no idea how much time Lord Greymount spent in his own suite, or whether he had enough business in the castle to keep him occupied elsewhere, but I did know one thing for certain—if I stayed in here like a meek little mouse, then I would certainly have no chance at all of meeting up with him. After he had taken his leave of me the day before, it had seemed clear enough that he had no intention of coming to see me again any time soon.

I set the book aside and rose from my chair. As I did so, I heard a knock at the door. At first, my heart leapt—but then I realized it must be the steward, returning to bring me some much-needed firewood. And if he did that, I would have no reason at all for venturing forth from my room, at least no reason that didn't sound very self-serving.

My grandmother had always made sure I did not curse. Nevertheless, several select words I'd heard the village men utter when they didn't think any women were around entered my thoughts. I pulled in a breath, however, then squared my shoulders and went to answer the door.

To my utter astonishment, it was Lord Greymount who stood there. He smiled, but I thought I detected a slight strain in his dark eyes, as if he had something else occupying his thoughts but wished to appear pleasant. "Good morning, Mistress Sendris."

"L-lord Greymount," I stammered, my composure deserting me at this apparition.

"I realized that our tour of the castle stopped rather abruptly when we came to the library," he said, apparently affecting not to notice my discomfiture. "I thought perhaps we could continue?"

"Of course," I replied at once. At least I had enough wits about me to know how I should answer him.

"It is quite chilly, however. I believe there is a woolen mantle in amongst the other items of clothing in that wardrobe. You may wish to put it on before you venture forth."

To be sure, I had noticed that mantle, but had pushed it aside when in search of a gown to wear, since I had not thought I would require it, confined within the castle's walls as I was. But I nodded and went to fetch it. For a moment, as I reached into the wardrobe to pull out the garment, I had the oddest fancy that my reaching fingers would instead find a cloak of white fur.

Of course they did not. I grasped the mantle of heavy dark blue wool and settled it about my shoulders. That did help somewhat, for even with the last of the fire I had lit earlier warming the room, it still seemed chillier today than it yet had during my tenure at the castle. That reminded me of the firewood, which most definitely needed replenishing.

"I need to let Master Merryk know that I have quite gone through my supply of wood—"

"It is no matter," Lord Greymount said. "When I inquired after you this morning, he told me that he would be bringing up some more very shortly. Now we can be out and away while he manages that task."

I was not sure why I did not quite like the idea of Master Merryk going into my room when I was not there. Indeed, it was not even my room, not really. Only a place I was borrowing for a time until I could return to the cottage I shared with my grandmother. And the truth was, I needed someone to bring up that firewood. I could only imagine his lordship's reaction if I offered to do it myself.

"That is very kind of both of you," I said politely as I shut the wardrobe and moved toward the door.

Master Merryk left my thoughts as I grew closer to Lord Greymount. Today he wore a doublet of warm wine-colored wool, and over that a long black cloak. I had thought him handsome before, but something in that color combination brought out the breadth of his shoulders, the warm undertones to his complexion and hair. My breath caught when he drew near, but then he stepped out of the way so I might move past him and out into the corridor.

He had been correct about the cold; I saw my breath mist into the air as soon as I left the warmer confines of my room, and I pulled the heavy mantle closer about me. "Does the castle usually get this chilly?"

"Not like this." For a second, he glanced upward, as if trying to divine what the weather might do next. "But it is still far better than being outside."

Of that I had no doubt. The wind was howling just as loudly this morning as it had been the night before. No human being could survive for long in those kinds of conditions, no matter how warmly they might be dressed.

"Well, I suppose if we walk briskly enough, we shan't notice," I said, hoping I sounded unconcerned by the prospect of taking a tour in the castle's unheated hallways. After glancing around and seeing that he was completely alone, I asked, "But where are your dogs? I would have thought they would enjoy this sort of exercise."

"In general yes, but they were rather wearied from their constitutional this morning in the courtyard, and are sleeping by the fire in my suite. It is not possible to strap snowshoes on a dog, after all."

His eyes twinkled as he said this, and I smiled up at him at the notion. Yes, I supposed it would be difficult for dogs to manage in this weather, even great beasts such as Doxen and Linsi. "Well, then we shall just have to do without them."

"That was my plan, yes." A pause, and then he offered me his arm. "So let us go forth, Mistress Sendris."

Once again I found my breath catching, but for an entirely different reason. Had he completely forgotten what had happened the last time we touched? I sent an uncertain glance up toward him, but I could see nothing in his expression save a mild interest.

Well, if he was willing to take the risk again—

I looped my arm in his, holding my breath the entire time. But nothing at all happened. Very well, something happened. A small, warm thrill passed through my body at standing so close to him, of having our arms linked, but it was nothing like the shock I had experienced when our bare fingers had touched on that first occasion.

Very strange. However, I was not given the chance to analyze the situation, for almost at once he began to move forward, saying he wished to descend one floor so we might visit the portrait gallery. I had to admit that sounded very grand, for I had never seen an actual painting in my entire life. One of the village boys, Alyk Lesiter, could sketch quite beautifully with discarded pieces of charcoal, but that was not quite the same as creating an entire picture with oil paints, which I had heard were very expensive. And to have an entire gallery of them?

We went to the staircase and went down to the floor beneath mine. Here, too, were corridors filled with closed doors, and I wondered why the place had been built on such an extravagant scale when so few people actually lived here. But perhaps matters had been different in the time of Lord Greymount's father, or his father's father.

The hall opened into a long chamber that seemed almost as if it ran the entire length of the building. One wall was comprised of windows only an arm's breadth apart, letting in a grey, wintry light. The other wall, however, had been hung with a series of paintings, carefully positioned so they did not directly face a window, and perhaps reflect its glare, or become faded by the sunlight.

Here, Lord Greymount let go of my arm so he might make an expansive gesture that encompassed all the room's contents. "Behold! Fifteen generations of Greymounts!"

His tone was slightly mocking, and so I had the impression that I was not supposed to be amazed. Perhaps he simply did not know that I had never seen a single painting before, let alone at least two or three score in a single space.

The portraits were of both men and women and, more rarely, a family grouping. Although my eye was unschooled at best, I thought I detected subtle differences as my gaze moved along the collection, since some appeared to be flat in nature and almost stylized, whereas the paintings at the far end of the gallery seemed to be more natural in their composition. Indeed, the last one, of a man who bore such a strong resemblance to Phelan Greymount that I thought he must be his lordship's father, looked so real that I wouldn't have been terribly surprised if he had winked at me.

"This is all your family?" I inquired.

"Yes, grandsires and great-grandsires, and—well, you get the picture. In a manner of speaking."

The pun was so poor that I couldn't help sending him a sideways glance, complete with lifted eyebrows. He grinned at me, and made a little bow.

"My pardon, my lady. Sometimes these things simply...slip out."

I decided it was best to give him a lift of my shoulders as I continued toward the far end of the chamber. Beyond the portrait of Lord Greymount's father—if he was truly the subject of the painting—I saw a blank spot. Turning, I sent his lordship an inquiring look.

"Yes, that one is for my portrait."

"You haven't had one painted yet?"

"It is not something I found particularly important." This time, he was the one who shrugged, although I noted something almost carelessly brittle about the movement, as if that portrait mattered to him more than he wanted me to know.

Somehow I knew it was better that I not pursue the subject. "I suppose it can be rather difficult to get portrait painters to journey all the way out here."

"Not as difficult as you might think. The Greymount family is known for paying well."

His frankness surprised me. For some reason, I had not thought that those of great birth, such as Phelan Greymount, would be open about discussing their finances. It was a topic we didn't bother to avoid in Kerolton, since everyone knew everyone else's business. But that was hardly the case here in Harrow Hall.

I attempted to sidestep the topic by saying, "Well, it seems clear enough to me that your family did hire very talented artists, whatever they might have been paid."

He laughed then, and shook his head. "How very politic of you, Mistress Sendris."

"Was it politic? I was only being truthful."

For a moment, he didn't say anything, only stood there and studied me. I found I did not much like being the subject of such a steady regard, and tried my best to look unconcerned, although within I worried if the cold light falling through those numerous windows revealed some of the strain from the previous evening's nightmares. At length he spoke, his tone musing. "I wonder that you have not had your portrait painted. Surely there are many artists in this land who would have leapt at the chance to have such a lovely subject for their work."

He had to be teasing me. Why else would he have made such a comment?

"I fear that we do not have many artists in Kerolton, my lord. And if we did, then I think they would devise more useful occupations than painting someone who spends her days working with dyes and herbs. In the summer, my hands are rather badly stained by the pigments, which I doubt is a detail that an artist would wish to reproduce."

His gaze fell to my hands, and before I could react, he had reached out for those hands and taken them in his. My heart began to thud painfully as he turned them over, then swept a thumb over my right palm.

"That's a pity," he said in low tones. "For they are very lovely hands, and suited for far more delicate occupations."

I swallowed. Once again, a strange warmth seemed to fill my body, and even though I knew I should come up with good excuse to pull my hands away, I found I could not. All I wanted was to stand there, so close I could smell the faint clove-like scent which drifted from his garments, and which must have come from the sachets he used to keep his wardrobe sweet-smelling. Unlike mine, his fingers were quite warm, even though our breath showed in faint white clouds every time we spoke.

Somehow I managed to speak. "It is honest work, my lord. I find nothing wrong with it. Indeed, it is quite enjoyable to wander the woods on a mild summer day while collecting my supplies. I would that it were midsummer now."

Still he kept hold of my hands, now twining his fingers with mine. Somehow I managed to keep myself from trembling, even though his touch sent a delicious thrill all through me. "Yes, I am sure you must be even lovelier in midsummer. Do you wear a crown of wildflowers on your head while you go to gather your leaves and bark...Bettany?"

His use of my given name was not lost on me. Up until this moment, we had always been quite formal. But there was certainly nothing formal about the way he stood so close, or the way he was gazing down into my eyes. I found I could not look away. Once more I saw that odd golden flicker in the depths of those dark irises, a gleaming glint which awakened a strange longing in me. I could not even say what it was that I longed for, only that its sole answer seemed to lie in the man who stood before me now.

A moment passed, and perhaps another. I could not say for sure, because time had no meaning for me when I was lost in his gaze in such a way. Everything about him seemed so very real, from the way a lock of black hair fell forward over his forehead, to the faint shadow of stubble that dusted his chin and cheeks. Unlike many of the men in Kerolton, he was clean-shaven.

Then his fingers tightened on mine, and he pulled me toward him. Surely he intended to kiss me. There was no other reason for us to be so close to one another, so close I fancied I could hear his heart beating within his breast, his blood pounding in his veins. Surely my own heart beat loudly enough that he should be able to detect it.

We were so very close, I could feel the warmth of his breath against my face. I stood still as a statue, knowing that I should pull away, and yet knowing I would do no such thing, that I would let him kiss me, no matter what happened next.

But in the next moment, I heard a rather ostentatious throat-clearing, and immediately Lord Greymount pulled away from me, a fierce frown tugging at his brows. Standing at the doorway to the portrait gallery was Master Merryk, whose attention seemed to be fixed on a point somewhere past the both of us. However, I knew he must have seen how close his lordship and I had been standing, how he had bent toward me, even if he was trying very hard not to show it now.

"My apologies, my lord," the steward said. "But the roof in the east tower has now also given way, and I thought you should come to survey the damage."

Lord Greymount muttered an oath under his breath. "If I must," he replied, irritation clear in his voice.

"Thank you, my lord. One of the men standing guard there was injured slightly, and I know it will do him good to see that his master has come to check on him."

Because Master Merryk had phrased it that way, I knew Lord Greymount had no choice now but to go and see to his wounded man-at-arms, and also to see how badly the tower might have been damaged.

Even so, he paused for a second, his gaze fixed on my face. Something in his eyes seemed to say, *We are not finished here.*

But then he gave me a swift but graceful bow, and said, "It seems I must take my leave of you, Mistress Sendris. You will be able to find your way back to your room?"

I nodded, as I was not sure I was capable of sounding entirely calm.

Master Merryk put in, "I brought you more firewood and tended your hearth, so I think you will find things quite comfortable there for you."

His unspoken meaning seemed to be clear enough—that it was not comfortable at all here in this unheated gallery, and I should get myself back to my room like a good, biddable girl. Right then, I was not feeling biddable at all, but I also knew this was not the time or place to argue with Master Merryk.

This time, I did reply, for I could tell the steward was expecting me to speak. "Thank you very much, Master Merryk," I said. "That was very kind of you. I am looking forward to warming myself by the fire." I paused so I could gather myself before adding, "And thank you, Lord Greymount, for showing me the portrait gallery. It was quite...educational."

And with those as my last words, I gathered my borrowed mantle around myself and went out into the corridor, past an amused Lord Greymount and also Master Merryk, who right then looked as if he desperately wanted to scowl at me but didn't quite dare to reveal his displeasure while in his master's presence.

Whatever happened next, I very much doubted that I wanted to get caught up in any of their battles.

~❦ Chapter Eight ❦~

As promised, my chamber was quite comfortable, a newly laid fire crackling in the hearth. Master Merryk had even left behind a small plate with a fresh-baked roll and some butter, both of which seemed very welcome to me in that moment. After I sat down and had a few bites of the roll, washed down with some water, I began to feel a bit more like myself.

Not entirely, however. I could never forget the look in Lord Greymount's eyes as he bent toward me. I had seen need there, and something else, something I couldn't begin to describe, although whether my overall inexperience with men was at fault here, or only the quite obvious fact that I did not know his lordship very well, I couldn't be sure.

Now that I was away from his intoxicating presence, I needed to calm myself and take stock. What did he intend? That is, although I was yet unaware of all the particulars of the act, I did have some idea of what was supposed to happen when a man wanted a woman. If he was an honorable man, he offered her marriage first. But certainly I was not so overcome by Phelan Greymount's charms that I could not think logically, that I could ever begin to believe he would ask me to be his wife.

Which meant he only wanted to bed me. Whether that desire sprang merely from the dullness of being cooped up here with no other company, and the realization that he had a rather pretty young woman near at hand, I did not know. Or rather, I didn't want to admit that most indisputable of conclusions to myself, although an impartial outside observer would have stated the obvious, that of course his wish to be with me stemmed only from my proximity, and not very much else.

However, I didn't want to believe that his attraction had such mundane roots. Perhaps my stubbornness to acknowledge the most likely scenario came from a need to believe myself more special than I truly was. But there had been that deep, golden glow in his eyes, a heat which seemed to stem from something more than merely casual lust. Then again, how much did I know about lust, casual or otherwise? Yes, I had been on the receiving end of some very unwelcome attention back in Kerolton, but the rude advances I'd suffered from Ilan Martis were very different from the way Lord Greymount had taken my hands and looked down into my face. I'd wanted him to kiss me.

Oh, how I had wanted that.

Before now, I had scorned my mother for her weakness in succumbing to the man who fathered me. I had always thought she should have pushed him away, should have told him she would not surrender her virtue to any man who wasn't her husband. In my mind, such moral fortitude had seemed like a simple thing, one hardly worthy of a second thought. But now that I knew a little of what it was like to be flushed with desire—even though Lord Greymount and I had yet to share a single kiss—I began to understand my mother somewhat better.

Would I be able to resist Phelan Greymount, if he were to approach me in my chambers tonight?

I told myself that he would do no such thing, that he had treated me honorably so far...but I couldn't be completely sure. Our acquaintance comprised barely a week, and during that time, we had not spent all that much time in one another's company. In fact, it was only during the last few days that he'd purposely sought me out. Something in his attitude toward me must have changed, but I couldn't think what.

Surely not a good word from Master Merryk. I had seen his face when he came upon us, and I certainly did not have to be a user of magic from days long gone to know what had passed through his mind in that moment. He had been pleasant enough when I wasn't a threat, but now that his lordship had shown an interest in me, the steward seemed eager enough to make sure I spent as little time in Lord Greymount's company as possible. I doubted very much that his happening upon us in the portrait gallery had been mere circumstance. Indeed, Master Merryk was probably chiding himself for not coming there with his manufactured emergency a few minutes earlier, before his lordship and I had even held hands.

Thinking of it again only made another shiver pass through me. I did want more. I wanted Phelan Greymount to kiss me, to warm me as he put his arms around me. Perhaps if we were able to spend more time together, to taste one another's kisses, he would come to see me as a woman he might marry, despite my low birth.

No, that was a foolish notion. I needed to hold on to what remained of my common sense and do what I could to retain what little reputation I had.

To what purpose? I thought then. *No man in Kerolton wants you for honorable reasons because of the taint of your birth. So what precisely are you saving yourself for?*

What, indeed.

I broke off another piece of bread and chewed it slowly as I considered my options. I could be cool and aloof the next time we met, and let him know that just because I was a woman alone here in his castle, that did not give Lord Greymount the right to treat me as he wished. Or I could be pleasant, but chatty and lighthearted, pretending that what had passed between us in the portrait gallery held no special importance for me.

Or....

Or I could abandon my caution and my fears, and see what developed between us. What was the worst that could happen?

The same thing that happened to many incautious women, I supposed. Would Lord Greymount acknowledge a bastard child, if matters should come to such a pass? I didn't have to imagine what the reaction would be in Kerolton. "Like mother, like daughter," they would say. And oh, what a disappointment I would be to my grandmother, even if I told her that the father of my child was none other than Lord Phelan Greymount.

I shook my head. I could not believe I was sitting here and calmly contemplating whether or not I should allow myself to become intimate with Phelan Greymount. *Phelan.* I rolled the name over in my mind, wondering if our small moment of rapport this morning was even enough for me to be presuming so much. He had taken my hands in his, true, and gazed down at me as no other man ever had, but I daresay there were many who would think that a rather flimsy basis for believing anything more significant might develop between us.

Restless, I went to the window, even though I knew I would see nothing else besides the snow falling, endlessly falling. I stared out into the pale grey light, thinking of what I would give to see even a single patch of blue sky, just one lone tree. Perhaps there was a wood of some sort on the other side of Harrow Hall, but here there was nothing except those endlessly rolling hills, their contours muffled beyond all recognition by the thick coat of snow they now wore.

The cold was palpable, although I could tell that the window was sealed well enough. Against a chill such as this, however, even the sturdiest of buildings must be challenged. Again I thought of my grandmother, and prayed that she'd gone into Kerolton as soon as she was able to see this was no ordinary storm. I couldn't know for sure, though. Commonsensical as she was, she might have thought she could ride it out, not knowing what was in store for her, and indeed all of the northland.

I pulled the heavy velvet curtains shut, since they did provide an extra bit of protection against stray drafts. And then I went and poked at the fire, stirring it up so it would send some more heat into the room.

If only Phelan Greymount were here to put his arms around me, to take away the cold that seemed to have seeped into my bones. I thought I could suffer this storm gladly, as long as I could do so in his company.

But he did not come to see me. The afternoon passed with agonizing slowness, and at length Master Merryk brought me my supper. We exchanged a few pleasantries, but I could tell from the set of his mouth that he was still not happy with me. For myself, I tried to act as serene and unconcerned as I could. That is not to say that I did not let out a sigh of relief once he had left my room, for I found it more difficult than I had thought to maintain such a façade. At least, though, he was gone, and I was able to eat my meal of venison stew in peace, although I wondered the whole time whether Phelan was eating the same thing, whether he was alone in his room, or whether he had gone down to share his supper with his men, so he might help to buoy their spirits during this difficult time.

I did not know, for I did not know him well enough to judge whether he would do such a thing or not.

That night I was not terribly eager to close my eyes and go to sleep, for I did not know if I would be visited by another terrible dream such as the one I had suffered the night before. For the most part, though, my slumber was deep and dreamless, the only vision entering my mind not really a dream at all, but rather a wisp of a remembrance, something about walking in a summer wood with the sunlight slanting through the leaves and a warm wind pulling at my loose hair. That dream did not seem terribly surprising; I was sure we all longed for the return of summer after suffering through so many days of storm. Nevertheless, when I awoke, I could feel myself craving that warmth, much the same way I'd craved Phelan Greymount's touch the day before.

A bath was brought up for me that morning, and although I was glad of it, I couldn't help experiencing a few pangs of guilt at all the work it must have taken to heat that water, let alone bring it and the heavy cast-iron tub up all those flights of stairs. The two young men who brought it were clearly among the household staff, and not the men-at-arms; they would not quite meet my eyes as they deposited the tub on the stone floor immediately in front of the hearth, then fled.

But since they had gone to all that trouble, I thought I should enjoy the bath, and indeed it did feel good to scrub myself clean, then sit by the fire and comb my hair to make it dry more quickly. Afterward, I selected a gown I had not worn yet, one in deep crimson with golden embroidery around the neckline and hanging sleeves. Even though I had been given leave to use these garments, it still felt strange to put them on every day and realize that they had once been worn by Lady Greymount, a woman who had never lived to see her son grown.

I knew it was foolish to hope that Phelan would come to see me today. No doubt Master Merryk would devise some other reason why his lordship's attention was urgently needed, even if the latest collapse of a tower roof had been more or less managed.

After that thought passed through my mind, I did feel somewhat ashamed of myself. For a man had been injured, even if the injuries he'd suffered were not life-threatening. And surely there were many factors involved in keeping the castle running, some of which must require its lord's input. I could not think only of myself when so many other people had far more important claims on his time.

So I picked up a book and began to read, although I found myself distracted, my gaze lifting far too often from the pages before me and wandering to the door. I had resolved not to look outside any longer, for the sight of the snow falling and the trackless white expanses that surrounded the castle were quite enough to send me into a fit of melancholy. I had begun to believe that this storm would never end, that I would be trapped here forever.

Ah, but at least you would be trapped with Phelan Greymount, I thought then, and I wanted to shake my head at myself. If it were only the two of us confined here, then perhaps I would be cheered by such a notion. But with Master Merryk keeping a watchful eye on us, I rather doubted we would be allowed very many intimacies.

Someone knocked on the door, and I was out of my chair in a flash, even as I laid my book down on the seat. I could not hope that it was Phelan, but at least an interruption by the two manservants to fetch back the bathtub would break up something of the monotony.

But indeed, it was the master of the castle who stood there, light dancing in his dark eyes and a smile pulling at his mouth. He wasted no time on a greeting, but said only, "Have you seen?"

"Seen what?" I asked, mystified, although of course I was thrilled beyond measure that he was here at all.

He pushed past me and went straight to the window, where he pulled aside the draperies. At once a beam of bright light flowed in, and my mouth dropped open. Recovering myself somewhat, I said, "Is that—?"

"Sunlight," he replied. "Come look, Bettany."

My heart was almost as warmed by his use of my given name as it was by the prospect of seeing the sun again. I hurried over to the window and stood next to Phelan. Sure enough, directly above the castle was a patch of bright blue sky, with a cheerful yellow sun shining through. Its reflection off all the acres of pure, unmarked snow was almost blinding.

I hardly dared to breathe for fear it would all disappear, like a dream fading just before waking. Or perhaps that was merely the effect of having Phelan that close to me once again. "Is the storm over?"

The smile he'd been wearing disappeared. "I fear not. This is a small break. You cannot see it from this window, but some fearsome clouds are gathering once again to the north."

"Oh," I said, unable to keep the disappointment from my voice. I should have known this beautiful burst of sunlight could not last.

"Do not despair," Phelan told me then, as his fingers wrapped themselves around mine. At once I could feel one of those welcome waves of warmth, even with the icy air slipping in past the casement. "We should enjoy it while we can. Come down to the courtyard with me, so we can at least feel some sunshine on our faces before it disappears again."

As much as that idea appealed to me, I couldn't help but think of some of the more practical disadvantages to his plan. "I believe you said the courtyard was piled high with snow, that not even the dogs could easily venture forth there."

"True. But did I not also say that dogs are unable to wear snowshoes, while we humans have been granted that ability?"

"'Snowshoes'?" I repeated.

The twinkle reappeared in his eyes. "Yes. Did you not tell me that you knew how to use them?"

"Well, yes. But those times I was dressed a bit more"—I hesitated, as I did not want him to think me ungrateful for the beautiful clothes he had allowed me to borrow—"a bit more plainly."

Phelan shifted his weight, then crossed his arms as he gave my current attire a careful inspection. Having him look at me so closely quite made the blood rise to my cheeks, and I knew there was no way he could not have seen my flush this time, not when we stood only a foot or so apart. "Ah, that," he responded. "I fear we have no simpler women's garments on hand, and I somehow doubt you would care to dress in one of the kitchen boys' clothes."

No, I most definitely would not. Why, the very thought of allowing anyone to see me so immodestly attired—I shook my head. "I fear that is not a proper solution. I will just have to muddle along in this gown and hope for the best. At least it is wool, not velvet, and so may survive a soaking along the hem better than some of the other dresses you have lent me."

"Very practical of you. Then let us hasten, so we do not miss our chance at seeing the sun."

Ah, that would be a tragedy indeed, after so many days of gloom and snow. I said quickly, "Let me get my mantle," and hurried over to the wardrobe so I might settle it about my shoulders.

Once again Phelan offered me his arm, and I did not even hesitate as I took it. Somehow it felt right for him to guide me downstairs thus. Perhaps it was not entirely charitable of me to hope that Master Merryk might see us with our arms locked together, and realize that his attempts to prevent Lord Greymount from spending time in my company had proved ultimately fruitless.

But I did not see the steward, nor anyone else as we descended to the ground floor of the castle. I noticed that Phelan led me along the opposite way from whence I had gone the day I had encountered his men-at-arms in the great hall. Perhaps he did so on purpose, so that we could avoid meeting up with any of them, or perhaps this route was better suited to our intended destination.

We did traverse a long hall, one that opened on a short gallery which appeared to border the courtyard. It seemed his lordship had counted on my agreeing to this expedition, for two sets of snowshoes, one a good deal larger than the other, waited for us there.

"Should I be gratified by your confidence that I would say yes to your proposition?"

Something flickered in his eyes at my use of the word "proposition," but he merely gave a slight lift of his shoulders and replied, "Let us just say that I would have been surprised if you had declined the opportunity for some fresh air and sunshine."

True, he had gauged my reaction well enough there. "It is a good thing that I am not some fragile court lady and am used to walking in all weather," I said as I picked up one of the smaller snowshoes and began to fasten the straps over my well-worn boots. After one or two instances of nearly tripping in the too-large slippers that had come along with my borrowed wardrobe, I had gone back to wearing my boots, which were not nearly as elegant but much more comfortable. Just as well, I supposed, for those dainty slippers of kidskin would have been ruined in less than a minute if subjected to the conditions outside. Indeed, I did not even know if one could put on snowshoes over delicate shoes such as that.

But my boots had trodden through winter's snowbanks and summer's thunderstorms, and I knew they would serve me well now. Phelan did not respond to my comment about fragile court ladies, instead sending me a quick grin as he worked on getting his own snowshoes fastened.

Soon enough we were both outfitted. I took one stride in my snowshoes and almost tripped because of the dragging hem of my gown.

"Some difficulty, my lady?" Phelan inquired in arch tones.

"Not at all." I had already guessed that I would have to choose between ease of motion or modesty, and so I grasped my heavy woolen skirts and looped them up through the belt of embroidered leather I wore, thus getting them more or less out of the way.

It was certainly a far more practical arrangement for tromping through the snow, but I could not miss the way Phelan's gaze flickered toward my exposed ankles and lower calves—clad in fine woolen hose, true, but still—before he glanced back up at me.

"Ready, Bettany?"

Oh, how I loved to hear him say my name! I had already begun to think of him as Phelan, but only in the privacy of my own thoughts. I knew I would never dare to address him so unless he gave me leave. And so far he certainly had shown no sign of doing so.

He did, however, chivalrously offer his arm after he had opened the door to the courtyard, letting in a blast of freezing air. It quite took my breath away, and I wondered how long he intended for us to stay outside, even though the sun was out.

Well, I supposed we could address that problem later. For the moment, it was enough to follow him out to the heavily drifted snow, stepping down two shallow stairs before we began to move across the smooth, heavily packed surface.

"We should be far lower than this," Phelan said as he led me out to the center of the courtyard. His breath came from his mouth thick as white smoke. "There are actually twelve of those steps, but the rest are buried."

I looked down, shocked, but of course I could see nothing of what he had described, only the unblemished snow on every side.

A flash of white teeth as he smiled at my astonishment. "It is quite amazing. The actual ground of the courtyard is some twelve feet below where we stand now."

"What will happen when it melts?" That was the first thing to come to my mind, especially since we stood in a spot where we were out of the shadow of the keep, and the sun blazed down strongly upon us, even though its light had no real warmth.

"There is a drainage system, but I suppose the gallery we came through will flood, as it often does when first the spring rains come to wash away the snow. You may have noticed that there were no real furnishings in that chamber."

I hadn't been paying that much attention to my surroundings—that was a difficult thing to do when Phelan Greymount held my arm—but now as I cast back in my mind, I thought I did recall that there was no furniture at all, and only heavy sconces of dark iron on the walls, with not a single painting or tapestry. "That is rather inconvenient."

"A fact of life in a place as old as this, I fear." He raised his head toward the sky, as if wishing to drink in the sun. In its fierce light, I could see warm tones come to life in his heavy dark hair, as well as the faintest of laugh lines around his eyes.

Had he ever looked more handsome? I could not say for sure, because he had nearly taken my breath away from the first moment I laid eyes on him. But there was something about the way he stood there in the sunlight, as though some care that perpetually weighted his shoulders whilst he was inside the walls of his castle had now lifted, if only for a moment or two.

"Is it so very old?" I asked, thinking that a neutral enough subject. I knew I could not keep gazing at him like that, for he would see at once how much I wanted him to turn toward me and take me in his arms.

But again that shadow touched his features, even as he shrugged. "Yes. You saw all those portraits in the gallery. The oldest goes back some three hundred years, when my great-great—well, there are a too many 'greats' to trouble myself with calling them all out—my grandsire was given a grant to build a castle on this land and keep the surrounding country safe from an invasion to the north."

"From frost giants and such?" I made sure my tone was slightly teasing, for I truly did not believe such creatures had ever existed. Ours was a prosy enough world now that magic had been driven from it, and I found it hard to put much credence in the sorts of tales that were generally told by the fire to frighten young ones into staying close to home.

"No, of course not. Those are old wives' tales, and nothing more than that. But there was a great threat in the north once, although I have not been able to find much in any of the histories about it. Something, though...something came from there, came from the dark and the cold, and was enough to make the early Marks of Eredor believe there was value in giving this land to those who would defend it."

A great shiver passed over me then, although I could not say whether its origins lay in Phelan's dark words, or merely because it was so dreadfully cold out in the courtyard, even with the sun shining down on us. The mantle I wore was warm enough, but I had no scarf or gloves. The chill began to work its way through the soles of my boots and on up my legs, and I shivered again.

"But we should go inside," Phelan said then, looking down at me solicitously. "It is far too cold to stay here any longer."

"B-but the s-sun is still out, my lord," I protested, stammering as my teeth began to chatter. "Surely it would be a very g-great waste to miss any of it."

As if to give the lie to my words, the bright sunshine dimmed, and I looked up in dismay. A cloud passed over the sun, followed by another. It seemed Phelan's prediction that this was only a small passing gap in the storm was beginning to come true.

"No, we must go in at once," he replied. "It would not do for you to catch a chill, and at least you did get to see the sun, if only for a few moments. Besides, your lips are turning blue."

"They are not," I began in some indignation, then stopped when I realized he was probably teasing me. "Very well," I continued with as much dignity as I could muster. "If you think we should."

"I do think it."

So we turned and began to make our trudging course back to the doorway through which we'd first entered. As I moved, however, putting one snowshoe with care in front of the other, my skirt started to slip from where I had it tucked into my belt. It fell just as I had begun to take another step. Before I could stop myself, the snowshoe tangled itself in the heavy woolen folds, and I could feel myself beginning to fall.

A gasp escaped my throat, and Phelan turned at once, reaching to catch me before I could tumble into the snowbank before us. Somehow his own snowshoe got caught in mine, and in the next instant, we were both falling, crashing into the hard-packed snow as we landed with him almost directly on top of me.

For the longest moment, neither of us moved. I was acutely conscious of his weight pressing down against me, the strength and heat of his body. His mouth was only a scant inch from mine, his breath warm even as it rose in misty white clouds around us.

Surely he should be pushing himself off me, should be apologizing for his clumsiness—even though the spill was really my fault—and helping me to my feet. But he did none of those things. He only remained where he was, staring into my eyes.

Then he muttered, "Dammit," under his breath, just before he brought his mouth down on mine.

It was cold, so very cold, but in that moment I was as warm as if I stood out in the hottest sun of midsummer. Heat flared all through me, rushing into my icy fingers and toes, a heat that seemed to be its strongest somewhere in my lower belly. Oh, gods, I wanted this, wanted his lips touching mine, his body pressed against me, his tongue tasting me as I opened my mouth to his.

I had never known it could be like this, this need that seemed to pulse along every limb, every nerve, every vein. My arms went around him, even as his encircled me. I began to move my leg, having a vague idea I wanted it to wrap around him as well, but the snowshoe defeated me, banging into his calf and quite ruining the moment.

Well, almost. He did lift his head enough to break the kiss, but his eyes were still hungry, fixed on my mouth, and a tremor went through me.

When he spoke, his voice was rough with emotion. "Are you hurt?"

Was I? In that moment, I could not begin to tell. The heat started to recede, and I realized how very damp and chilled I was. But aside from one throbbing elbow where most of my weight appeared to have landed, I seemed to be more or less unharmed.

"No," I said, although my voice shook. I cleared my throat and added, "Perhaps a small bump on my elbow, but that is all."

With a groan, he pushed himself off me and got to his feet, managing his snowshoes with far more skill than I would have been able to. Then he extended a hand, and I took it. I did not reach a standing position with quite the same grace as he had, but a moment later I was back on two feet, albeit covered in snow.

"You must come inside at once," he told me. "Can you walk?"

In truth, my knees trembled somewhat, but I doubted that had very much to do with the fall I had just suffered. "Yes, my lord. I am fine."

"Stop it with that," he commanded. "You know you must call me Phelan now."

Although my feet were so cold I could no longer feel my toes, I went warm all over at those words. "Yes, my—Phelan."

He pulled me to him then and kissed me again. I forgot everything—my discomfort, the way the sun was now truly blotted out, the snow that began to fall all around us, lightly at first, but thicker and thicker as the kiss wore on.

"Yes, I am your Phelan," he said, still in that rough voice, as if he, too, had been overtaken by an emotion he could hardly explain. "But come."

Before I could react, his arms had slipped under me, and he lifted me from the snow and carried me to the doorway which led into the bare gallery where we'd put on our snowshoes. There, he deposited me on the floor and bent to undo the straps on the wicker and leather contraptions.

"There is no need for you to do that—" I objected, rather appalled that he would take such a subservient stance.

"Yes, there is. You are chilled through, and your gown is soaking. I would not wish you to bend over and become faint."

His tone would not allow any argument, so I subsided. And truly, it did feel good to have him minister to me thus, for it was not enough that he removed my snowshoes. After he had taken off his own snowshoes, he unclasped the cloak from his throat and put it around me. Its warmth helped to ease some of the shaking that had begun to wrack my body, and I smiled at him.

"Brave girl," he said. "Now I will take you to your rooms, and see that another hot bath is brought up for you. And you must rest, for I will never forgive myself if you should become ill because of our little...escapade."

The way he said the word made me worry that he was not as happy with this sudden alteration in our relationship as I had thought he was. Something in my expression must have shifted, for at once he bent and placed his lips on my cheek, then murmured, "Do not fret, my dear. I have no regrets...and I sincerely hope you do not, either."

"None," I told him.

He kissed me again, and his arms were around me as he lifted me and took me from that place, carrying me all the way up the stairs to my chamber. I wondered what would happen if Master Merryk should see us thus, but it seemed he was occupied elsewhere in the castle, and we reached the room that had become mine without encountering anyone at all.

Once we were inside, Phelan shut the door and hastened to the fire so he might build it up, since it had burned down almost to embers during the time we were gone. "Come and sit by the fire, Bettany," he said. "Warm yourself here, and I will go and summon your bath. And then...." He let the words trail off there, and watched me carefully as I limped over to the chair he had indicated and sat down.

"And then?" I echoed, wanting to hear what his response would be, yet somehow fearing it as much as I wished to know what it was.

"And then you will come and have dinner with me," he said. "I will make sure a great fire is built for you, and you can amuse yourself by feeding Linsi and Doxen table scraps."

His tone was light, and I knew I must take my cue from that. "Indeed? I cannot think that is something Master Merryk would much appreciate it."

Perhaps Phelan guessed that I was not talking about the dogs, at least not entirely. His eyebrow lifted, and he said, "Damn Master Merryk," just before he bent and kissed me again. It was over too swiftly, and then he offered a slight bow and was gone.

As for me...well, all I could do was sink down into the chair, and press my fingers to my lips.

Phelan Greymount had kissed me, and my world would never be the same again.

Chapter Nine

Alas, I was not to have that dinner with the master of the castle. Even before the manservants arrived with my hot bath, I had begun to shiver and shake, chilled beyond measure, although I had stood before the fire the entire time, hoping its heat would penetrate my sodden garments and begin to warm me.

I took that bath, thinking surely soaking in the hot water would help to rid me of the cold that had sunk into every bone, every muscle, but it did very little. By the time I had climbed into a fresh chemise and drawn a shawl around me, my teeth were chattering, and my flesh had begun to break out into goosebumps. It seemed to take every ounce of strength I possessed to stumble over to the bed and climb beneath the covers.

Master Merryk found me thus, after I did not answer the knock at my door from the servants who had come to fetch the bath away. He took one look at me, laid a heavy hand on my forehead, then informed me I must stay in bed, that I was burning with a fever.

Burning? Instead it seemed as if all my limbs were encased in ice. Not that I had any true experience of what a fever was supposed to feel like, since this was the first time in my life I had ever fallen ill. The steward went and stirred up the fire, but to me it did not feel any warmer in the room. Still my teeth chattered, and his expression was grave as he said he would go to inform Lord Greymount of my condition, and would bring me some warming broth.

I wanted to protest, to say that I was supposed to have dinner with his lordship in his chambers, but the words did not seem able to force themselves past my trembling lips. All I could do was give a weak nod and pull the covers even further up my neck. Soon afterward, Master Merryk went away and I fell into a fitful doze, slipping into darkness, then awaking with a start, unsure as to where I was. At that point, I still retained enough of my faculties to recognize the carved mantel, the heavy draperies of dark blue velvet, but still I was nagged by a sense that I should be someplace else, that there was something I needed to do, although I could not recall in that moment what it was.

Eventually, the steward returned with a heavy stoneware bowl in his hands. Seeming to realize that I could not take the spoon myself, he was able to tip a few mouthfuls of broth between my lips before I shook my head at him. The taste of it nauseated me, although it had smelled savory enough when he entered the chamber.

Expression grave, he set the bowl down, then once again laid his hand on my head. After murmuring something about fetching a tincture of willowbark, he went away, and I closed my eyes again. More drifting in and out of sleep, before Master Merryk entered the chamber and contrived to slip a few spoonfuls of something quite nasty-tasting between my lips. I sputtered and coughed, although within the tincture—concocted with some kind of heavy liquor, I surmised—I could taste the bitterness of willowbark tea, which my grandmother had always used to treat my grandfather's fevers and headaches. I had tried some of it once, wanting to know what it was that made my grandfather always screw up his face in distaste when he had to take it, and that was quite enough to cure me of ever wanting to drink it again.

After Master Merryk gave me the willowbark tincture, my world became quite black. I would have said that I merely slept, but the oblivion which claimed me seemed deeper than that. From time to time, I would claw my way to the surface, enough to see the firelight and the deep lines around Master Merryk's eyes as he bent to force more of the tincture between my lips. Always afterward, though, I would slip away, not knowing how many hours or possibly even days had passed since the last time I had gained even an ounce of consciousness.

Once I thought I heard the deep tones of Phelan's voice outside my door, as if he had some conversation with the steward regarding my condition, but I could not make out anything of what they said. And while I normally would have found the sound of his lordship's voice comforting, now it seemed only to agitate me, as if to remind me of something I had lost, something I had tried to reach out for, only to have it ripped from my fingers just as they began to close around it.

In the darkness, I found myself running, my breath coming in heavy, labored gasps. It was cold, so very cold that I could not feel my hands or my feet, could barely tell that I still breathed. But no, of course I was breathing, for the world seemed to grow lighter, and I saw my breath rising in great white clouds all around me, even as the landscape became more clear.

These were not the rolling plain-lands that surrounded Harrow Hall, but the forests I had grown up in, the ones which surrounded my grandmother's cottage. All the trees were thickly covered in snow, and snow fell around me as well, covering the trail of footprints I had left in my wake. How would I ever find my way back?

But no, that was a foolish thought, was it not? For even with its blanket of white, I recognized the woods I traversed now. If I kept walking, soon I would arrive at the cottage that was the only home I had ever known. Why on earth would I want to go back the way I had come, when my destination lay only a few minutes away?

For some reason, though, my heart sank at the thought that all traces of my passing might soon be gone. I realized then that I did not wish to go to the cottage. I wanted to turn and run back to Harrow Hall, and to the shelter of Phelan Greymount's arms.

That choice appeared to be denied me, however, for in my dream my feet kept carrying me inexorably forward, along a path I had trodden so many times that I knew I could traverse it while blindfolded if need be. And there, through the rippling curtains of snow, I could see the cottage take form, dark and somehow squat, diminished in my eyes, perhaps, because I had now seen the grandeur of Harrow Hall.

But through the windows I spied the warmth of firelight, and I hastened forward, mindful now of the way my wet skirts slapped against my ankles, of the snow that clung to my woolen mantle. In that moment, all I could think of was a chance to be warm once again, to be away from this endless snow and biting cold.

As I approached the cottage, the front door swung open, and I saw my grandmother standing inside. She held a cup of some steaming liquid, and held it out as I entered and shut the door behind me.

"Some broth, my dear," she said.

Something in her voice sounded altered, scratchy and hoarse, but perhaps she suffered from an ague, no strange thing in these days of cold and snow and damp. In that moment, I could only think of downing the hot cider, or perhaps warm broth, that the cup contained.

So I reached for the cup she held. As my fingers started to close around it—and to touch her fingers as well—I saw that her hand began to change, began to grow bristling grey fur, her fingernails stretching into claws. I jerked back in shock, but she dropped the cup and grasped my wrist with her clawed hand, keeping me from pulling away.

And her eyes—they were not the kindly blue I remembered, but amber-gold, glowing balefully into mine as her face somehow began to shift and distort and lengthen, nose becoming a snout, lips turning black and thin as they lifted to reveal sharp, gleaming teeth. A snarl emerged from her throat.

A scream burst from my own throat in that moment. Not caring how her claws might score my wrist, I wrenched my arm away, began to run for the door. I expected those same claws to bury themselves in my back, but for some reason I was able to grasp the doorknob and stumble outside, where my footprints had already disappeared. No matter. I would run and run and become lost in these woods before I would allow myself to be trapped here with this thing that was a counterfeit of my grandmother.

From within the trees I heard the howling of many wolves, howls that were answered by the creature inside the cottage that had once been my home. Where to run? No direction seemed safe, but I must go somewhere. I bolted to my right, as it sounded as if there were fewer wolf calls coming from that way.

More than ever my heavy skirts dragged in the snow, and I almost lost a boot in a particularly deep snow drift. But I knew I must keep running, that if I stopped, I would surely die. The howling grew ever closer, and I recalled the dream I had had some days earlier, when the wolves had chased me down in the snow and set upon me.

Was this a dream? It felt far too real, but then, so had the other. My thoughts chased around one another, circling me just as the wolves had begun to. I could see them now, shadowy shapes slipping in and out of the trees, elusive as mist but far more deadly. What they waited for, I did not know. Some signal shared only among them, I supposed.

My breath swirled around me like smoke as I struggled onward, knowing that there would be no escape, no way of surviving this encounter. The wolves toyed with me, no doubt, delighting in my fear, in the frenzied beating of my heart, the pounding of the blood in my veins.

Blood they would taste soon, unless I could find some way to awake from this nightmare.

And then they lunged, moving in from all sides. One of them seemed far larger than the others, and I realized it was the wolf that had once been my grandmother, for on one of her claws I saw the gleam of silver and knew it to be the wedding band my grandfather had placed on her finger so many years ago. I could only thank the gods that he had not lived to see what had come of her.

Their teeth caught the hem of my cloak first, pulling me to the ground, and then they were upon me, jaws closing on my arms and legs, blood spilling out onto the snow. I screamed, although I knew there was no hope of succor, no hope of any-one coming to my aid, not when there was no one else around for miles and miles.

Screaming, my throat raw...

...and then there were arms closing around me, warm, human arms, and his voice calling my name, bringing me back to myself.

"Bettany! *Bettany!*"

I blinked, and saw that I was in my borrowed bed, and it was Phelan who sat there next to me, his arms pulling me close, so warm, so safe. In that moment I did not think of the impropriety of him holding me so when I wore only a chemise, or that he should not have been in my chamber at all. I could only drink in deep breaths of the sweet clove-scent from his garments, and let myself feel warm again for the first time in days.

"Oh, Phelan," I sobbed.

His arms tightened around me. "My dear, what was it? I could hear you screaming all the way to the staircase."

At another time, I might have been mortified to have made such a scene of myself. In that moment, however, I was only glad that he had been passing close enough to hear me. Was it possible to die of fright while trapped in a dream? One would think such a thing could not be possible, but I could feel how painfully my heart was thudding away in my chest, and such a notion did not seem as farfetched as it might once have.

"A nightmare," I murmured. "That is all."

He pushed a damp lock of hair away from my brow. "It must have been a very terrible nightmare. Do you wish to tell me of it?"

As much as I welcomed his comfort, I did not think that I cared to tell him of the horrible visions that had visited my sleep. "I—I don't recall that much," I replied, hoping the lie was not too terrible. "Something about running in the dark and the cold."

"That does sound distressing." He stroked my hair again, and I found my terror ebbing away, gone now that he was here. Then he touched a hand to my forehead and went on, sounding relieved, "I believe your fever has broken. That could have caused the nightmare, I suppose. Sometimes these things must peak before they can finish running their course."

"Is my fever truly gone?" Now that I had had some time to regain my composure, I thought I did feel much improved, an improvement which could not be solely attributed to Phelan's presence.

He laid his hand against my forehead once more. I had to fight to prevent myself from letting my eyes close at the bliss of his touch. "You are still warm, but nothing like you have been these past few days."

"Days?" I repeated, aghast. How long had I lain here, slipping in and out of oblivion?

"Two days, two nights," he replied. His hand slid down to my cheek, caressing, and a shiver went through me that had nothing to do with the fever I had suffered. "You were very ill. But Master Merryk kept dosing you with his willowbark tincture, and told me I should not worry too much, that overall you were strong and healthy and should pull through in time." He paused then and smiled at me. "Which it seems you have. You still have some convalescing to do, though."

"Is the storm still with us?" I asked, for I could see nothing through the thick velvet curtains which covered the windows.

The smile faded. "I fear it is. We have had a break or two, like the one when we went out to the courtyard, but they never lasted more than half an hour at most. The snow has quite covered those steps we descended."

Which meant the drifts must have risen another two feet or so. I wondered how long we could possibly continue like this, whether the snow would go on and on until it buried the first-floor windows, and began to pile its way up to the second, and so on and so on until the entire castle had disappeared from view and we were all buried inside it.

What Phelan had seen in my expression, I could not say, but clearly I must have evinced some measure of dismay, for he took my hands in his and held them tight. "Bettany, I will not lie to you and say we are not concerned, but the situation is far from disastrous. We had a great store of food laid in, and we will be able to survive, even if this blizzard should last another fortnight. We all hope very much that it does not, but it is nothing to trouble yourself over. The very worst you have to fear is being confined here with only me for company."

Those words elicited a chuckle from me, albeit a rather rusty-sounding one, and he raised my fingers to his mouth so he could kiss them one after the other, as if concerned that he might neglect even my pinky. The touch of his lips against my skin brought forth another delicious shiver, and I wished I had not been so very ill, that I might be able to kiss him as he had kissed me in the courtyard.

But then I realized what a fright I must look, and how it was rather dreadful that he should see me thus, even though at first I had been very glad of his presence. Resisting the impulse to tear my hands away so I might attempt to smooth my tangled hair, I said, "I can think of far worse things than being restricted to only your company, Phelan Greymount."

"Indeed? I must confess that I am glad to hear you say so. Now, though, I think you should rest. I will send word to Master Merryk that you are much improved. Do you think you could eat something?"

Now that he had asked the question, I realized how ravenously hungry I was. Not so strange, after all, when I had gone more than two days without any real food. "Yes, I think so," I told him. "Perhaps some broth, and bread."

"And some warm cider, I think. I will have Master Merryk see to it right away."

"I do not wish you to take any particular trouble—"

Phelan stopped those words right away, holding up a hand as he said, "You are no trouble, Bettany Sendris. You must know how very much you have come to mean to me. So do not be meek, or humble. Let me take care of you."

What on earth could I say in response to that? My cheeks heated, but not from a fever this time. To think that a young woman such as I could have made such an impact on him! I nodded. "Thank you, Phelan. I do admit that it feels quite wonderful to have you wishing to take care of me."

A smile spread over his face then, and he took my hand once more, kissing it before he hurried out in search of the steward. For myself, I could only fall back against the pillows, that encounter quite exhausting me after such a long time lost in fever. As wearied as I felt, however, I could not help grinning as I stared up at the ceiling.

I meant something to Phelan Greymount, and if it had required my illness for him to recognize that fact, then I could not regret too much those days I had spent in my sickbed.

Chapter Ten

*A*ny hopes I might have had of a quick convalescence were dashed by the steward, however. He came to see me, and laid his hand on my brow and looked at the whites of my eyes, and although he said I did seem a good deal improved, I should not dream of rising from my sickbed for at least another couple of days.

"I understand your caution," I told him, "but truly, I feel myself quite recovered, and not dizzy or weak at all."

"And how far have you tried to walk?" he asked, expression stern.

An embarrassed flush touched my cheeks then, for I had only gotten up to use the garderobe, hidden in its curtained alcove off to one side of the chamber. I did not wish to confess such a thing to him, even though of course we all had to attend to such functions during our daily lives. "A few feet," I replied.

"Which is good, but it is better to be careful." A pause, as if he was weighing what to say next. I watched him with some surprise, because he was not the sort of man to show much hesitation, had always seemed very assured to me. "Mistress Sendris, I took care of you because I have had some small training in these things, but I am no physician. If you were to over-exert yourself too soon, you might suffer a relapse and make yourself truly ill. And then there would be very little I could do to help you. For you know there is no chance of summoning a doctor in this kind of storm."

Of course he was correct. In that moment, I was rather ashamed of my impatience. I had only thought of my eagerness to see Phelan, and had not considered what getting out of bed and wandering around the icy corridors of Harrow Hall might do to impair my slow but steady improvement. "My apologies, Master Merryk," I said. "I should have thought of that. I will make sure to stay in bed until you deem it safe for me to be up and about again."

An expression of relief passed over his features then, one so obvious that for a second or two I wondered at his solicitude. Was he truly so concerned for my well-being, or was there some other reason why he was glad that I would be confined to my bed for a while longer?

Because he does not wish you to see Phelan, I thought then. *His lordship might not care about your mean birth, but it is clear enough that his steward thinks you are not at all suitable. If you are kept away from Phelan for a few days, perhaps his ardor will cool, and things will go back to the way they were. Or at least that is what Master Merryk hopes.*

I did not dare utter these truths—if truths they were—aloud. No, I hid them deep within my heart, knowing I was in no position to make any sort of accusation against the steward.

I could not even hate him for his attempt to keep me away from Lord Greymount. In a similar situation, I might not have acted so very differently. Any halfway objective observer would have said that I was far beneath him, both by birth and my current station in the world.

But I did not want to dwell on that unfortunate discrepancy. Phelan had said I had come to matter to him, and that was the important thing. He was lord here; whatever he decided to do when it came to this strange attraction between the two of us, that decision should be up to him, and not Master Merryk.

All these thoughts passed through my mind in what must have been the blink of an eye, for it seemed that the steward noticed no hesitation in my manner. He offered me a smile I did not for one second believe, then said he would be back to check on me later in the day. I nodded and hoped I looked grateful, and was more than relieved when he let himself out.

As soon as the door shut, I gathered up the heavy woolen shawl that had been lying across the foot of the bed and drew it around my shoulders, then pushed back the covers and slid down to the floor. Yes, my legs felt rather wobbly, but I held onto the edge of the bed until I thought myself more or less steady. After that I took a cautious step toward the hearth, followed by another. There. That wasn't so bad, although I was glad to sink down into the chair which had been placed near the fire—and equally glad that the floor was covered nearly from wall to wall by an enormous Keshiaari rug, and so my feet had suffered no risk of touching the icy stone.

My heart did pound from even that simple exertion, and I took in a breath. Perhaps Master Merryk's estimation of my condition had not been so far off after all. But I had just proven to myself that I could walk farther than the garderobe, and I vowed to do so multiple times, in order that I might strengthen myself and be ready that much sooner to have my long-delayed dinner with Phelan.

And if my speedy recovery should surprise the steward, well, I did not think I would shed too many bitter tears over his discomfiture.

I was careful, though. I made sure I was always back in bed anywhere close to the time when I might expect Master Merryk to check in on me, and I meekly swallowed the broth he brought up, and also that terrible willowbark tincture, even though I knew my fever had gone and I had no real need of it. Each time he would tell me that I needed more rest, and I did not bother to argue.

Phelan came to see me several times, but his visits never lasted very long. Perhaps the steward had admonished him not to tire me, or I would have to remain in bed that much longer. Each time he came to see me, though, he remarked on how improved I was, and how he had no doubt that I would be up and about in no time.

To which I would nod and smile, but reveal very little. For I thought it best to surprise him, to show that I was entirely recovered, and that perhaps his steward's judgment on the matter had not been entirely accurate.

Several days passed in such a way. As the third evening headed into full dark, however, I thought it time to prove to Phelan that I no longer needed to be confined to my bed. The steward had come and gone with my meager meal of broth and bread, and I knew I should not be disturbed again until the following morning. Perhaps the thought of venturing out into the dark castle should have daunted me, but I believed that I recalled the way to Phelan's chambers well enough, and surely they must have lit some of the candles in the hallway sconces so the servants might take their lord his supper. If I was very lucky, I might get to see him before they even arrived; I had gotten the impression that the steward brought me my meals sometime before the rest of the household sat down to dine.

After listening carefully to make sure I could not hear any footsteps out in the corridor, I got out of bed and selected the wine velvet gown I had worn on my first day here. Once I was dressed, I went over to the little table with its attendant mirror and brushed my hair, then pinched my pale cheeks to bring some color to them. Biting my lips several times also made them flush redder, and I inspected my reflection carefully. Yes, I thought that should do rather well. I did not think I looked like someone who had spent the greater part of a week in her sickbed. In truth, I was not, because once my fever broke, I felt more or less restored to myself. But certainly the steward did not know that.

I unlatched the door and let myself out into the hallway, then paused and looked from side to side in order to determine that I truly was alone. Certainly there was no reason for anyone to be about in this wing of the castle, but I thought I should take care nevertheless.

As I had hoped, candles did burn in some of the sconces, and so I was able to see well enough to make my way over to the great stairwell and ascend the three levels to the story where Phelan's suite was located. By the time I had reached that floor of the castle, I did feel myself somewhat winded. It seemed I was not quite as recovered as I had hoped. No matter. I was still able to walk more or less normally, and the descent to my chamber would of course be much easier than the climb here had been.

I did not think it was all exertion that made my heart beat more quickly as I approached the double doors which opened onto Phelan's chambers. Would he be angry with me for coming here unannounced and uninvited, or instead worried that I had put too much strain on myself for coming all this way so soon after my fever had broken? I had to hope that he would only be relieved I was so recovered, and also happy that I so desired to see him alone, I had not thought of myself or my still fragile health.

When I approached the door, however, I stopped, for I heard not one, but two voices within. Phelan's, and Master Merryk's. My heart sank, for I had not even considered that the lord of the castle would not be alone in his suite.

But then I held my breath, for their words were coming to me clearly enough that I could hear what they were saying. It was wrong, but I could not prevent myself from listening to their conversation. No, I did not press my ear against the door, but I did stand very close, and held myself there as quietly as possible.

"...taking a very great risk, my lord," Master Merryk was saying.

"What risk?" Phelan returned. "I have spent all this time with her—been more intimate with her than you would like, no doubt—and I have suffered no ill effects. How can such a thing be possible, save that she must be the one?"

A silence, during which I dared not stir even the slightest bit for fear they might discover that someone was listening at the door. "I do not know," the steward said, his tone heavy with doubt. "But I cannot understand how this is possible. After all this time—and those previous incidents—"

"What is there to understand? We both have the evidence before our eyes."

"*You* have the evidence, my lord. I am still not entirely convinced."

A muffled noise followed that statement, although I could not guess whether it was caused by Phelan getting up from his chair, or perhaps because he had merely made a sound of disgust at his steward's words. "Would you be offering these arguments if she were high-born?"

"I will not lie, my lord. Of course my heart would be easier if Mistress Sendris were not a mere peasant."

"Her grandmother is the daughter of a tin merchant."

"Oh, well, then, that makes all the difference."

I wondered at the steward taking such liberties, for the sarcasm in his words was plain enough for anyone to hear, even coming through the door as those words were. But then, I did not know all that much about the relationship between the two men. Master Merryk was a good deal older than Phelan, and I had inferred that the previous Lord Greymount had died fairly young, so perhaps the steward had taken on something of the role of a father to the young, orphaned lord. Even so, I was surprised that Phelan did not take the older man to task for what he had just said, or at least at the manner in which he had uttered the remark.

"It makes some difference," Phelan said, his voice uncharacteristically mild. "But beyond that, Bettany herself confessed to me that she does not know who her father was. *No one* knows, apparently. So because of that fact, and because I have not reacted to her the way I should have, I am led to believe that he must have been one of *them*. Which makes her perfect."

Them? Who on earth was he talking about? There was some mystery here, something I could not begin to guess at, for I had no context. Of course, such a lack did not prevent me from listening further. Perhaps if they kept talking, they would offer more enlightenment.

Another pause. When Master Merryk spoke next, reluctance was clear in his every syllable. "I suppose that is possible. It does offer the only plausible explanation. But she truly has no idea of who her father is? Her mother never said anything?"

"From what Mistress Sendris told me, it seems the mother disappeared as well when Bettany was very young. She said nothing to her daughter, or to her parents, of the man who had fathered her child."

"That would make some sense, if the father was truly one of *them*."

"So you see why I have come to my decision. The meanness of her birth means nothing to me, not when she herself is the answer to this curse that has plagued me ever since I came of age. And besides—" He stopped himself there, and I wished I could see his expression, could have a better chance of determining what he might be thinking. Up until this point, it seemed that all his defenses of me sprang only from what I was—whatever that might be—rather than who I was. Did he care for me at all, or was I only a convenient answer to this "curse" of his? I recalled then the touch of his lips on mine, the heat in his kisses, and told myself he must care, that no man could kiss a woman in such a way if he did not care a great deal.

But then, my experience of men was not large. Perhaps such things were easy enough to counterfeit. I knotted my hands in my skirts and strained to hear what they would say next.

"And besides, at least she is young and pretty?" Master Merryk said dryly.

"More than pretty. She is a very beautiful young woman. But her beauty only made matters more difficult for me at first. I needed to know that I was not making this decision merely because I wanted her."

While these words did not precisely make me relax, they did do something to lift the cloud that had begun to darken my thoughts. Although it seemed obvious that Phelan had some overriding reason as to why he had made his "decision," he also thought I was beautiful. He wanted me. It was something to be desired by a man like Phelan Greymount, even if that desire was only a fraction of his current motivation.

"And you are not making this decision based on that?"

"No." A pause, and then Phelan added, "At least not entirely. At any rate, I need to act now, while she is still here with us."

"Since we have seen no sign of the storm stopping any time soon, I believe there is not much chance of Mistress Sendris leaving us in the near future. But if your mind is made up—"

"It is."

"Well, then. It seems some preparations will be required. When do you plan to speak to her?"

"Tomorrow. It grows late, and I would not wish to intrude on her rest."

Shame flooded through me at his words, at his believing that I was safely confined to my bed, rather than wandering these drafty halls and listening in on his private conversations. True, this particular conversation involved me, and one might say I had a right to know what Phelan and his steward were discussing. But I could not find much relief in that particular rationalization.

Guilt fled next, giving way to panic, as I heard a creak that must have been Master Merryk getting up from his chair. He said, "I should look in on her one last time this evening, to see if she requires anything else. Her health is much improved, but there is a pallor to her cheeks that was not there before she took ill."

"I thank you for your solicitude," Phelan replied.

I, on the other hand, most certainly did not thank him for it. I knew I must be gone at once. Gathering up my skirts, I fled down the hallway and thence to the stairs, which I rushed down so precipitously I almost tripped, and only saved myself from a tumble by grasping the handrail. And then it was down to my room, and a mad rush to climb out of that gown and have it safely stowed in the wardrobe.

The covers had barely settled themselves beneath my chin when I heard a knock at the door. "Mistress Sendris? Are you yet awake?"

"Y-yes," I called out.

Master Merryk entered the room, his gaze immediately going to me where I lay in bed. His eyes narrowed. "Are you quite well?"

"I—yes, that is, I thought I had improved a good deal today." I didn't dare pull the sheets and blankets and embroidered coverlet any further up, for then they would have covered part of my chin. All I could do was hope that the dim candlelight in the room would not reveal too much of my expression, which I was sure must have been as guilty as that of a child who'd been caught stealing sweets from the larder.

"Hmm." He came closer to the bed, and laid a hand on my forehead. "You seem quite flushed, Mistress Sendris, and your breathing is somewhat labored. I hope that your fever is not attempting to reassert itself."

Of course it wasn't. No, the only thing truly the matter with me was that I had just rushed down several flights of stairs and had run down a long corridor to get here before he did. I could not confess to such a thing, so I only said, "Well, I did get up and walk to the window earlier, so I might see if there were any signs of the snow letting up. Perhaps that was it."

"You should not be getting out of bed," he told me, voice stern. "You must be guarding your health, so you will recover that much more quickly."

"I am sorry, Master Merryk," I said. "I will be more careful from now on."

"Good. Now sleep, and we will see how you fare on the morrow."

I nodded, my expression as meek as I could make it. That response seemed to mollify the steward, for he offered me a faint smile and let himself out. Once he was gone, I shut my eyes and allowed myself to release a relieved breath.

That had been far too close. I must take more care in the future, for I did not want to jeopardize the connection that had begun to grow between Phelan Greymount and myself... even if that connection was based on secrets he apparently did not wish to reveal to me.

Although Phelan had intimated in his conversation with the steward that he planned to speak to me sometime the next day, I had no true idea of precisely when. I did not wish to have this momentous discussion—whatever its topic might be—while I was lying in bed, wearing a chemise and with a shawl draped around my shoulders. On the other hand, he would surely find it suspicious if I were up and about, and dressed as if I had known he was going to come see me.

Surprisingly, it was Master Merryk who came to my rescue. When he brought me breakfast, he asked if I was feeling better, and if I thought I might be able to sit up for a bit. "For I believe his lordship would like to look in on you," he said, "but would not wish to do so while you were still in bed."

Clearly, Phelan had held his tongue about the way he had come to my aid when I was consumed by that nightmare, and had said nothing about how he had sat on my bed and held me until I was calm once again. Not that I had really thought he would divulge something of such a personal nature, but I could not help but be relieved that those moments were ours alone, and nothing anyone else knew of.

"I think I can manage that," I said, "as long as it is not too lengthy a visit."

"No, it should not be overly long."

This reply only piqued my curiosity that much further, although I knew I should not question Master Merryk on the subject. Whatever it was that Phelan wished to say to me, I would find out soon enough.

I said that sounded very well indeed, and the steward left soon after, telling me that his lordship would be up in an hour or so. As soon as he had gone, I went to the wardrobe and got out the wine-colored dress I had worn so briefly the night before, thinking that Phelan should get some chance to see me in it.

Once again I went through the ritual of brushing my hair and pinching my cheeks to give them some color. Despite my agitated start to the evening, I had slept well enough, and thought my appearance had improved, with most of the hollow look gone from under my eyes. As I stared at my reflection, I wondered again as to the purpose of Phelan's visit. A suspicion had begun to grow in me, one I did not want to give conscious thought to, for if I were to let that suspicion grow into a coherent shape, I might see it for the ridiculous thing it truly was.

When he knocked, I went to let him in calmly enough. I did not want him to see the anticipation that had begun to rise in me, even though I tried to tell myself it was entirely without cause.

"Bettany," he said, a warmth in his voice that seemed to send thrills all through my body. "You are looking remarkably well."

"Thank you, Phelan," I replied. "I am feeling much better."

"I can see that. So it seems that Master Merryk's strictures have had the desired effect."

"It would appear so." I gestured toward the hearth, where I'd placed the room's one upholstered chair, and the plain wooden one that accompanied the dressing table. I could only hope that I sounded natural enough, for I did not want Phelan to see the trepidation that had entered my thoughts ever since Master Merryk had arranged this meeting. "Would you like to sit by the fire?"

"That sounds excellent. After you, my dear."

Out of instinct, I began to make my way toward the wooden chair, for of course it would not do to take the better one when it should have been reserved for his lordship's use. But he lifted an eyebrow at me, and I ducked my head before offering what I feared was a foolish smile, then sat down in the upholstered seat.

Smiling as well, he took the hard little chair opposite me. He was so tall that he appeared to dwarf the fragile piece of furniture, which had clearly been fashioned with a lady's smaller frame in mind. Once he had settled himself, he said, "I suppose you are wondering why I wished to speak with you this morning."

"Is it a cause for wonder?" I asked. "I had only thought you wished to check on my condition, and see for yourself how improved I am."

"Well, that, yes." For the first time he appeared somewhat ill at ease, a condition so unlike him that again a suspicion grew within me, the one I hadn't dared to give a name. "And something else."

"Indeed?" My mouth felt dry, and I wished I had asked the steward to leave a flagon of cider and some cups for us. I had the pitcher of water provided for my personal use, but only the one silver goblet, and that didn't seem to suit our current situation at all.

"Indeed." Phelan leaned forward and took my hands in his. Although we sat fairly close to the fire, his fingers felt nearly as cool as mine. But I thought that not so very extraordinary, considering how cold most of the castle was, and how long we had labored under the effects of this unending storm. "I know we have not known one another for so very long...."

"Some nine days," I supplied.

A flash of a smile, one that warmed in a way the fire could not. "Ah, I see you've been keeping count. Yes, nine days. Some would say that is a very short span, but it has been enough to convince me."

"Convince you?"

His fingers tightened around mine, even as his eyes met my gaze. We sat there for a long moment, neither of us speaking. And yet in those dark depths I saw another flash of gold, echoing the leaping flames of the fire beside us. "Convince me that I wish to have you with me always. Bettany, tell me that even when this storm breaks, you will remain here with me. Tell me that you will stay here and be my wife."

For the longest moment, I could not find the strength to respond. I could only stare at him, at the fine long nose, the thin but beautiful mouth, the strong lines of his jaw. It was as if I had never seen him before, as if those words he had just spoken had thrown his entire face into sharp, perfect relief.

So it seemed those mad suspicions of mine were actually correct.

When I replied, my voice shook. "You would ask this of me, Phelan? But you are a great lord, and I am no one."

"I believe you said that to me the first time we spoke," he said. "I did not believe it then, and I most certainly do not believe it now. You are not *no one*. You are Bettany Sendris, the choice of my heart. Do you deny me that choice?"

In those words there was a hint of the arrogance I had heard when we first met. But that did not bother me. Why should a man of his birth and his looks and mind not be somewhat arrogant? Indeed, hearing that self-assurance was something of a relief. It meant he had not changed so very much...even if he had changed enough to consider taking a low-born young woman for a wife.

"You know I cannot deny you," I said. "Perhaps it is not ladylike for me to speak of such things, but there are many who would say I am not a lady at all. So I will tell you the truth, Phelan Greymount. I will say yes to you, and stay with you. Not because you are a great lord, or because I will become the lady of this castle. It is because you kissed me, and I knew from our first kiss that I could be with no one other than you. Does that make me shameless?"

He laughed then, and stood, pulling me to my feet as well. "Honest, rather, and I can think of no other quality more valuable in a wife." A pause, and he looked down at me, eyes glinting. "That is, besides passion. And I have kissed you, and tasted you, and know that you are certainly not lacking in that quality, either. So kiss me now, my darling, and seal our pact."

With one swift movement, he drew me against him, his mouth claiming mine. We kissed for a long while, kissed as we should, with the heat of the fire warming us, and a different and even more splendid heat coursing through our veins. After a long moment, we broke apart, and he smiled down at me. "We will begin with the preparations at once."

And it was only then that it truly came to me that I was to be Phelan Greymount's wife, and the lady of Harrow Hall.

⚜ Chapter Eleven ⚜

Phelan had spoken of preparations, but truly, I did not know precisely how grand those preparations could be. It saddened me to think that I should be married without my grandmother present, and although I tried to tease my betrothed and tell him that I would not disappear the moment the storm finally ended, he would have none of it, and insisted that the wedding should take place as soon as possible.

"As soon as possible" meant the day after next, apparently, a prospect which did little to ease my roiling thoughts.

"And I would have had it even sooner than that," he told me, "if it were not that Master Merryk has said you should have that extra day to make sure your strength is all that it should be."

"You must thank him for his solicitude," I replied, knowing I must sound fully in possession of myself, even though my body seemed to run both hot and cold at the thought of being his bride. "For I know I would wish to have my full strength on the day I become your wife."

"This is true. I would not wish for you to become too easily wearied."

No, I supposed he would not. I was a young woman of little experience, but I knew enough to guess what Phelan was thinking about. He would not want a wife who was exhausted on her wedding night.

At the thought, a small shiver passed over me, one that had very little to do with the chilly air seeping in around the edges of the window, where I had paused once more to see if the snow had yet decided to stop...which of course it hadn't. I had kissed Phelan, and knew the effect those kisses had had on me. I could only imagine what it would be like to be completely intimate with him, to know what it was to be his wife.

When he left me after that particular exchange, I found myself wondering once again about the "curse" he had spoken of, and how he was so certain that marrying me was the one thing he could do to break it. Not that I even believed in such things; the wizards and witches of yore might have hurled such things at one another during their magical battles, but those with such power in their veins were long gone, with only we simple mortals left behind. There were those who did seem cursed in one way or another, like Lahrn Westover, whose cows always seemed to want to wander off and disappear for days, or have their milk go bad—or give birth to a two-headed calf on one noteworthy occasion—and yet I'd always thought they were merely the object of some spectacularly bad luck. A curse, a *true* curse, in the manner that Phelan had spoken of his, was something which simply should not exist.

And yet I dared not question him on the subject, for then I would be revealing that I had listened in on his conversation and heard things that most assuredly must have been meant for Master Merryk's ears only. No, the best I could do was reassure myself that, whatever this curse might be, Phelan had also stated most clearly that he desired me, thought me beautiful. He wanted me, and wished to spend the rest of his life with me. What woman could question such simple ardor?

But it was not so simple. I knew that, but I felt myself powerless to stop the tide that seemed to be sweeping me directly into Phelan Greymount's marriage bed. For who was I, after all, save a simple young woman of mean birth and few prospects? If there had been anyone from my village present to hear my protests, they would have laughed until they cried. Who would be foolish enough to refuse marriage to such a great lord?

Not I. If I had disliked him or found something objectionable about his person, perhaps then I might have tried to assert myself...not that such protests would have done any good. The Phelan I knew was not the sort of man to force himself on a woman, but if his character had been different, I doubted he would have scrupled at such a thing, if the woman in question had something he wanted. And no matter what else I might think on the subject, I could not deny that I had something Phelan wanted. What that something precisely was, I had no idea, and I rather doubted he planned to tell me.

The morning of my wedding day dawned, and a bath was brought up so I might prepare myself. My breakfast that day had been more than usually sumptuous, with fresh-baked bread and crisp bacon and a saucer of delicious spiced apple compote.

When he'd brought me my meal, the steward had apologized for the utter lack of a serving woman to help me prepare for the momentous event, which would occur later that afternoon.

"It does not seem fitting to me that the future Lady Greymount should be left to fend for herself," he said, "but of course there is no one here who could take on the task."

"You needn't worry yourself over the matter, Master Merryk," I replied. "I have never had a serving woman to assist me at any time in my life, and I fear I would only feel awkward if one were here to help me now. I can manage very well on my own, I assure you."

In answer, he had smiled at me, and yet I thought I saw him wince slightly, as if he did not care to be reminded of my lowly origins. Very well. I could not change who I was, and Phelan did not seem to mind. That should be the only thing of importance in this situation, not the steward's opinion of my birth.

But he merely said, "That is very good to hear. His lordship did bid me bring you this, that you might wear it this afternoon. It belonged to his mother, and it was his wish to see you in it."

With that he took a flat box from where it rested on my breakfast tray and lifted the lid. Inside was a diadem of silver, delicately wrought with thin rays of metal rising from a slender band, and from each of those rays dangled a crystal that danced and sparkled in the firelight. I had never seen anything so lovely in my life, and my breath caught. Phelan expected me to wear that beautiful ornament, I who had never even owned a copper ring?

Of course he does, I thought then. *For you are to be the lady of Harrow Hall, and no doubt will have many fine things. You will simply have to pretend that you are accustomed to such luxury.*

"It is very beautiful," I said. "Thank his lordship for me and tell him that I will be honored to wear it."

"I will," Master Merryk said gravely. "And now I shall leave you to your breakfast. Lord Greymount will see you in the great hall at four o'clock this afternoon. I will bring you there."

"Thank you." How could I sound so calm? Inwardly, I was quivering with nervousness...and anticipation. Beneath that anticipation, however, I could not help experiencing a stab of worry. So Phelan intended to have the ceremony in that enormous hall I had seen when I stumbled upon his men eating there. Did that mean his men-at-arms would be in attendance, witnesses to our joining? I did not think I cared much for the idea of such an audience at our nuptials, but then, I realized he might not have much choice. Perhaps it was better that they see our joining, and understand that I was now the lady of the castle, not some stray Phelan had taken in and given shelter from the storm. Very well, I was that stray...but now I would be so much more.

Master Merryk took his leave of me then, and I forced myself to sit down and eat, even though my appetite seemed to have deserted me for the moment. I did not want to face those men again, even with Phelan at my side. But I knew I must. Surely they would not be so foolish as to do or say anything untoward while the lord of the castle was present.

Or so I tried to reassure myself. When the two young men brought up my bath, I fancied that the glances they sent me were more curious than ever, but I knew that reaction was due to my own nerves more than anything else. I took as much pleasure as I could in that bath, for it did feel good to get warm all the way down to my toes. This time I had not been provided the bar of yellow soap that had come with the bath on the other times I had used it, but a bottle of a liquid that smelled of chamomile and mint, and which was wonderfully refreshing.

There was really only one choice for my wedding gown. All of my borrowed dresses were lovely, and yet there was the one I had thought too fine to wear, and had left pushed to one side of the wardrobe. Now I drew out the gown of blue and silver, with its collar of white fox fur, and laid it reverently on the bed. The fact that it was a style long gone out of fashion mattered nothing to me; it was beautiful, and far lovelier than anything I had ever thought I would wear on my wedding day—not that I had really expected to wed at all, considering my dismal experiences with the men in Kerolton.

The dress had gotten slightly musty, and I left it to air out while I went and sat by the fire, twisting my wavy hair around my fingers so it might dry into ringlets rather than its usual unruly mass. I had taken such care in the past on one or two occasions, such as the midsummer dance in the village square. Most days I did not have the leisure to spend so much time on my hair, but I wanted to look as perfect as possible for Phelan. I wanted to look like a lady.

Once my hair was dry, I went to inspect the gown. The wrinkles had relaxed somewhat, and I thought it should pass muster, especially in the gloomy expanses of the castle's large ground-floor hall. I drew it on, thankful that this gown laced up the side, most likely because of the large fur collar. The soft fur settled against my neck, warming me, and I carefully disposed my hair over it, not wanting to muss the curls I had so carefully created while I sat by the fire.

The only thing left was the diadem. I stood in front of the mirror and then gently placed the ornament on top of my head. The silver work was so delicate that I barely felt it resting against my hair, and I vowed to take care and not accidentally dislodge it while I was moving about. I had no hairpins or other means to secure it, but I thought as long as I didn't move too quickly, it should stay in place.

And then I stood there, gazing at my reflection. Surely there was no way anyone would be able to tell that I had not been born to wear such garb, for I knew I did not look at all like myself. A stranger stared out of the mirror at me, an elegant young woman with carefully arranged curls and a certain sparkle in her dark eyes that was echoed in the glinting crystal drops of the diadem she wore.

Would Phelan even recognize me? I barely recognized myself.

There was no use looking out the window to see the angle of the sun. I had already pushed the curtains aside and glanced out earlier that day, and, as ever, the snow still fell, swirling around the towers of Harrow Hall, continuing to build up on every side. I doubted one could even push open the main gates of the castle, so buried were they. Indeed, I was rather surprised that Phelan intended to have the ceremony in the hall, located on the ground floor of the structure as it was. But I did not pretend to know very much about the castle's layout, save the barest idea of where his rooms lay in relation to my borrowed chamber.

I swallowed, realizing then that his suite would also be mine after this day had passed.

Master Merryk had left me an hour candle, that I might know the exact time when I should descend to the hall. He had apologized for that makeshift as well, explaining that he would be busy with preparations, and so could not be spared to come fetch me. I accepted this explanation readily enough, even though at the time I did wonder why he could not send one of the manservants to come and get me at the appointed hour. But no matter. In a way, this was better. I did recall enough of the castle's layout to remember how to get to the hall, and descending alone would allow me a chance to compose myself as best I could without having to put on a brave face in the presence of a stranger.

A glance at the candle told me that the hour was almost here. I went about the room, tidying up everything I could, making sure that my borrowed books sat in a neat stack on the table where I had left them. After the ceremony, I would have no reason to come back here, except to fetch such items I might need. But this would not be my room any longer, and I wanted to make sure it was as ordered as when I had first come here.

The wax dripped down to the line drawn across the candle's surface. I could not delay any longer, but must go to meet my soon-to-be-husband.

It was as if in a dream that I left my chamber and closed the door behind me. Flames flickered in the sconces along the walls. Not too many, just enough to safely light my way. The uncertain light only heightened my sense that this could not be happening, that I must have conjured all this up while in some sort of fevered dream.

But the cold stone floor felt real enough beneath my feet, and so did the icy bite of the air against my face. In my haste, I had quite forgotten to take up my borrowed woolen mantle. For a second I hesitated, wondering if perhaps I should go back to fetch it. Then I decided not to waste the time, that the hall had a great fireplace, and most likely would be filled with people for surely Phelan would wish to have witnesses to our nuptials. That chamber would most certainly be warmer than these corridors. And after that....

Well, after that I would have Phelan to keep me warm.

Nevertheless, I hurried down the stairs, heavy skirts held in my hands so I might not trip. The activity did help to warm me, although I made sure my descent was not so precipitous that I risked dislodging the precious diadem I wore.

When I swept into the hall, I almost stopped. For I did not see the crowd I had been expecting, but only several men—Master Merryk; a tall, lean man-at-arms whose elegant cloak and burnished breastplate seemed to indicate he was the leader of the household guard; Phelan himself. Where everyone else was, I had no idea. Perhaps Phelan had decided it would be better to only have a few witnesses after all, and not subject me to the scrutiny of the rest of his men.

As soon as he caught sight of me, he moved in my direction, hands outstretched. "My Bettany! How beautiful you are!"

A great fire was roaring in the enormous hearth, but it was not its heat that sent a flush to my cheeks. "Thank you, my lord. I did want to please you."

"Oh, you have." His eyes raked me up and down, and I had little doubt what was passing though his mind in that moment.

And why should it not? I would soon be his wife, after all, and there was certainly nothing wrong with having impure thoughts about one's wife. "You are looking very fine today as well, my lord," I responded, hoping I sounded dignified and gracious, as befitted the lady of the castle.

At any rate, my compliment was nothing more than the truth. He wore a doublet of dark green velvet, one I had never seen before, and a heavy silver chain set with faceted jet was draped over his shoulders. Truly, he looked so grand that he might very well have been setting forth to the Mark's courts in Tarenmar.

But no, he was not going anywhere, not with the storm that still raged around us. He had donned this finery for his wedding day, and my heart warmed that he had taken such trouble. Whether that effort had been made for my benefit, or because it would have looked odd to Master Merryk and the captain of his guards if he had not, I could not say.

I had to leave off my pondering, however, for he took me by the hand and led me closer to the fire, where the other two men waited for us. The question had come to me before this, but I had not had a chance to ask it of Phelan until now.

"And who will marry us?" I murmured. "For I see no priest here."

"Not precisely," he replied, in the same undertone. "But Collyer here studied to be a priest of Inyanna, and even took his vows, before he realized that was not a life for him, and that he wished to carry arms instead. Even so, Inyanna's blessing was not taken away from him, and so he is able to perform the ceremony."

This explanation did calm me somewhat, even while I thought the situation rather irregular. *Of course it's irregular,* I told myself. *You are marrying a man far above your station after knowing him for not even a fortnight. There is absolutely nothing "regular" about this situation at all.*

That was true enough, although I knew we had gone too far to stop anything now. Not that I would have tried, even if such a thing had lain within my powers. For all the strangeness that surrounded us, I wanted to be Phelan's wife, no matter what else happened. Indeed, there were times back in Kerolton when a priest was not able to make the journey to our little hamlet, and so the eldest person in the village read the vows. Such ceremonies were still considered binding. At least this Collyer had undergone the training to be a priest, even if he had changed his mind about his true vocation.

"That is convenient," I said, then wondered whether I should have kept the comment to myself. I did not wish Phelan to think that I was being sarcastic. Truly, I had said the first thing that came into my mind, for I was desperately attempting to sound calm and unworried, despite my racing heart.

If he thought anything amiss about the remark, he gave no indication. My words only brought forth a smile to his lips, one that made my knees go weak, and he nodded slightly. "Yes, it is convenient." Straightening, he turned toward the two men, both of whom had been standing there in silence, waiting for us to be ready.

Although Phelan had spoken no words, Collyer seemed to understand that the time had come. He moved toward us, then gave a grave nod. When he spoke, his voice was measured and calm, still with the smooth intonations of his priestly training. Whether he used the same tones when commanding his men, I had no idea, but at least I did not have to worry about being barked at while reciting my marriage vows.

It was an old, old ceremony, one that went so far back people said it had been handed down from the gods themselves. I had no way of knowing if that was the truth or not. In my mind, I thought it rather something conjured by men so they might be certain of their wives' fidelity, but of course I had never dared to utter such a heretical opinion out loud. Despite my doubts as to the ceremony's origins, I could not help but find myself relaxing somewhat as I heard the familiar words once again, words I had never thought would apply to me. But here I was, standing next to Phelan as Master Merryk stepped forward with the ritual cloth and handed it to Collyer so he might wrap the piece of fine linen around his lordship's and my wrists, symbolizing the manner in which we would be eternally bound to one another.

After Collyer removed the cloth from our wrists, he went to the hearth and dropped it into the fire so it might be burnt to ash, with no way of knowing which part had been bound to me and which had been bound to Phelan. I had heard that in true temples, a special brazier was reserved solely for this purpose, but back home the linen was always placed either in a bonfire or in the hearth of the home where the ceremony was being performed, depending on the season.

And then it was time for Phelan to place his lips on mine, to seal the bond that had been created between us. As soon as our mouths touched, my entire body flushed with heat, even though the kiss was quite chaste, very unlike the impassioned embraces we had previously shared. Well, I could not fault my new husband for his restraint; we did have his steward and his chief man-at-arms looking on, and such a display would not have been appropriate.

"Congratulations," Master Merryk said as soon as Phelan and I had parted. "The cooks have been preparing quite a feast for you, my lord and my lady. We will have it brought up to your suite."

Even though I had prepared myself for this new reality, it was something to think of Phelan's sumptuous chambers as being my new home. A shiver went through me, although my husband did not seem to notice.

"Thank you for that, Master Merryk," he said. "I will escort my new bride there, and we look forward to what you have to serve us." He turned toward me and offered his arm, and I took it. With no more ceremony than that, he led me out of the hall and to the staircase. We had not ascended more than a few steps before he slanted an amused glance down at me and spoke again. "I trust that was not too terrible? I know you wanted to have your grandmother here to see you wed, but of course that was not possible. However, I also had the idea that you would not much appreciate having my men-at-arms as your witnesses, and so I kept the ceremony modest."

"That was thoughtful of you, Phelan," I replied. "I must confess that I was not looking forward to marrying you in front of all of them. And since we had Master Merryk as our witness, nothing else was required."

His dark eyes glinted, taking on a certain warmth I had begun to recognize. "Well, nothing besides this." Then he did bend down and kiss me, thoroughly this time, his arms around me, his mouth open to mine so we might taste one another again. The world seemed to sway and dance, and I was glad he held me so closely, or else I might have lost my balance. When he lifted his mouth from mine, he added, "That was how I wished to kiss my beautiful new wife. But I did not wish to shock my steward, and so I forbore until we could be alone."

"That was...wise," I said, sounding more than a little breathless. I found I didn't mind all that much. I wanted Phelan to know he took my breath away.

"Come, my dear," he said then. "It would not do for the servants to find us here on the steps, skulking like a footman stealing a kiss from one of the scullery maids. Let me show you your new home."

Only in this house, there are no scullery maids, I thought as Phelan led me up the stairs to his apartments. *Will that change, now that I am his wife? And what of a lady's maid?* For I had a vague notion that the wife of someone as grand as Phelan Greymount of Harrow Hall should have a woman to attend her, although I had no idea what I would do to keep her occupied. I could already manage my hair, my wardrobe. What else would be needed?

I pushed those concerns aside, however, as Phelan guided me down the corridor that terminated in the double doors to his suite. He pushed open one of those doors, saying, "All this is for you."

When I gazed inside, I could not help letting out a gasp. Yes, I had seen these rooms before, but now they blazed with candlelight, which was reflected in the polished surfaces of the furniture and lent an extra warmth to the heavy velvet curtains at the windows and the hangings on the walls.

All those candles, when we had been snowbound for so many days. I could not help but wonder at the extravagance of the sight, even as my heart leaped that Phelan would do this for me.

"I can see it in your face, my dear," he said. "It is nothing to concern yourself over. We had a great store of candles here, far more than we could use all winter. I wanted to give you some light, when so much in our world has been darkness lately."

What could I say to that? Nothing, not when he had made such a gesture on my behalf. But my gratitude and love must have shone forth from my face, for he bent and kissed me deeply, his hands cupping my face as if he held the most precious of jewels between his palms.

"Now, my love," he told me, "let us go in."

Chapter Twelve

There was wine, of course, which we drank from fine goblets of exquisite glass that had come all the way from Sirlende. I did not have much experience with that liquor, for in Kerolton we did not have such luxuries. But that wine...it slid down my throat, heavy and dark, promising even greater abandonments later that night. Perhaps I should have been more cautious about drinking it, but why? I was here with Phelan, my husband. I did not have to worry about offering the wrong impression or compromising my virtue. That "virtue," such as it was, would be abandoned to him soon enough.

But first there was the promised dinner, brought up by Master Merryk himself and two of the manservants, a feast that required all three of them to carry in the covered dishes and platters and arrange them on the sideboard in the dining area. For there was a dining area, one off the sitting room where Phelan and I had held our first conversation, on a day that now felt years in the past rather than barely more than a week. Linsi and Doxen already waited there, eyes gleaming, although they were too well-trained to get underfoot, and instead lay curled around one another in a corner, clearly hoping they might be treated with some scraps once the steward had gone and they were no longer under his watchful eye.

Phelan and I also waited off to one side while Master Merryk and the other two servants bustled about, and then we were left alone, in a room shimmering with candlelight and filled with the aroma of all manner of delectable food. By then we had already drunk some of the wine, which had been poured into a decanter, but Phelan added an inch or two to my half-empty glass, then pulled out a chair.

"My lady," he said.

It was strange to hear him call me that, and stranger still to realize that anyone I met from now on would address me in a similar fashion. When I returned to Kerolton to see my grandmother, I would be there as Lady Greymount, not simple Bettany Sendris. Assuming I ever went back to the village that had been almost the entirety of my existence until a short week ago. Something about this storm made it seem as if the rest of the world had somehow disappeared, that Phelan and I and the rest of his household floated in a dream-castle adrift in a sea of snow. A mere fancy, I knew; eventually, even this monumental blizzard would spend itself, and the world would become real once again.

I shook off the notion, and smiled up at Phelan as I took my seat. "Thank you, my lord."

He sat down, mouth quirking somewhat. "You are very formal, my lady."

"I think many would deem this a formal occasion, my lord."

Those words elicited a laugh, and he raised his glass toward me. "I suppose they would," he said, "but I hope you will not *always* be so formal."

"We will have to see, I suppose," I replied. But I couldn't prevent my lips from curving upward in a smile even as I spoke.

"Ah," he said. "That smile is not formal at all. In fact, I think many would say it was not even proper. I had no idea you had such a wicked streak, Bettany."

"Do I?" I inquired, my expression all innocence. "No one has ever accused me of that before."

"Which only reinforces my belief that all the men in your village are dolts, or at the very least deficient in their eyesight. But no matter. I suppose I should be grateful for their stupidity, as it preserved you for me."

This last was said with such good humor that I couldn't help but laugh, even as I wondered what those same men would think if they ever found out that their lord had called them stupid dolts. Well, since Phelan was their master, I supposed they would keep their opinions to themselves. All the same, it did amuse me somewhat to think of their discomfiture, considering their less-than-noble treatment of me. I had to confess that I would rather enjoy seeing the expression on Master Wisegrot's face, once he realized that the woman he'd thought barely worthy of him was now married to the lord of Harrow Hall.

"But enough of that," my husband went on. "We should eat before this food gets cold. I do not want to think of Master Merryk and the rest of the servants going to such trouble, only for us to waste their efforts."

"Of course," I said quickly. "It all looks marvelous."

Phelan smiled and lifted several pieces of venison, dripping some sort of richly scented sauce, onto my plate. Almost as soon as the meat touched the metal surface, Linsi and Doxen moved from their place in the corner and deposited themselves so close to my feet that I could feel Doxen's tail thump against the hem of my gown.

This behavior was rewarded with a stern glance from my husband, but because he said no word to send the dogs away, I guessed that he was not a particularly stern taskmaster when it came to making sure his pets were not underfoot during mealtime. While some might have thought less of him for being so lax, I found myself glad that he allowed the dogs to remain close by. In the past, my grandmother had scolded me for giving tidbits to the cat, saying that by doing so, I made him far less likely to chase rats and mice. Her remonstrances had some logic to them, I was forced to admit, but I did tend to ignore her advice and continued to feed Malkin treats when I knew my grandmother wasn't looking.

"Do you mind them?" Phelan asked after he had finished heaping all sorts of delicacies on my plate, including a mound of mashed turnips swimming with butter. "They will go back to their corner, if you wish."

"No, please have them stay," I replied, bending down to scratch behind Linsi's ears with my free hand. "They are not in the way at all. I only hope you will not scold me too badly if I feed them the occasional scrap."

"I will not scold you if you show me the same forbearance. They have been my constant companions for nearly five years now, and so I fear I may have been more indulgent with them than I should."

"How could I rebuke you for showing them affection? That can only make me think better of you, not worse."

His gaze warmed as he looked at me, and he set down his fork so he might lift his wine glass in salute. "Then let us drink to showing affection, shall we? For I know I do not wish to be a distant husband to you, the way some are."

I did not think there was much risk of that, if the way he had kissed me previously was any indication. But I raised my wine glass as well, then said, "I hope you will be able to show me such a thing very soon."

My remark caused him to laugh, and once again I thought I saw that golden glint in his eyes. "There it is again," he said. "That wicked streak. Ah, how you please me, Bettany."

Blood rushed to my cheeks as I thought of the several ways such a remark could be interpreted. I supposed I would find out soon enough exactly what he had meant. To cover my discomfiture, I asked, "Did you ever think we would be here like this when I stumbled upon your doorstep?"

"No," he replied frankly. "But then, when you were first brought in, I fear you did rather resemble a drowned rat. It was only after you were on the mend that I realized what a rare and lovely creature the gods had seen fit to send me."

How I was supposed to reply to such praise, I had no true idea. Truthfully, I was not much in the habit of receiving compliments, especially from men. Those who had wanted me had no time for wooing, apparently thinking I should be grateful to receive any sort of attention at all. Although I had done my best to forget it, Clem Wisegrot's singularly inelegant proposal rose in my thoughts then. *You should be my wife,* he had said, *for no one else will have you, and, despite your other shortcomings, your face is pleasant enough.*

The memory was enough to make my mouth twitch, and Phelan raised an eyebrow. "What is it, my love?"

"Nothing," I replied. "Nothing important, that is. I was just thinking of how Clem Wisegrot had made sure to mention my shortcomings when he asked me to be his wife."

"How very peculiar. I cannot say that I have an inordinate amount of experience on the subject, but I am fairly certain that it is not generally considered good form to insult a woman when asking her to marry you."

I could only chuckle. "I suppose Master Wisegrot believed himself to be such a catch—and so far above me—that he saw no need to sweeten the offer. But the expression of consternation on his face when I refused him was well worth the sting of the original insult."

"As I said earlier, dolts. Foolish dolts." Phelan drank some of his wine before adding, "But I am sorry you were subjected to such a speech."

"It did not sting overmuch. I was used to it by then."

My husband's dark, level brows pulled together, and his mouth tightened. "When I hear you say things like that, I find myself wishing to go to this village of yours and raze it to the ground."

Although I knew of course he would never actually do such a thing, I found myself rushing to Kerolton's defense. "Oh, but they are not all like Master Wisegrot! Amery Willar is a very fine man, and so is Master Branner, the miller. And Mistress Overlin makes very good pottery, and my grandmother herself—"

"Enough," Phelan cut in with a laugh. "You do not need to enumerate all their singular qualities. I believe you when you say there is enough in Kerolton that is worth saving. All the same," he went on, mouth curling slyly, "I doubt you would shed too many tears if Master Merryk were to find some reason why Clem Wisegrot's taxes might be raised *ever* so slightly."

Indeed, the prospect did amuse me somewhat, although I felt compelled to point out that such an abuse of power was not at all desirable. "I would really rather you did not," I said. "For one thing, it is not fair to raise a man's taxes simply because he is lacking in tact."

"Or taste, or comprehension," Phelan interjected. "But do go on."

I feared I could not argue with my husband's assessment of Master Wisegrot's character. However, I said, "For another thing, once the unfortunate Master Wisegrot learns that I am the new Lady Greymount, he will undoubtedly do the sums in his head, and realize that his unfortunate tax situation might have a great deal to do with the way he insulted me in the past."

"I think you give his powers of comprehension greater credit than they deserve," my husband replied. "But no matter. I would not wish to make you uncomfortable, my dear, and so I will let the matter lie. Instead, let us speak of more pleasant things. How are you finding your dinner?"

"Excellent," I said, for indeed, everything I had tasted in between the rounds of our current conversation had been quite delectable. "Really, I've never had anything so wonderful as this venison…and my grandmother fancies herself a very good cook."

"Is she?"

"With what she has to work with, yes."

Phelan's eyes glinted. "And you?"

I shook my head. "My talents do not lie in that direction, I am afraid. I cannot burn water, as some say of particularly poor cooks, but I do not seem to have that special knack of making a few simple ingredients taste far better than they should."

"It matters not, for, as you have seen already, I have an excellent cook. No, my love, I fear the only thing you will need to do is keep me amused…and look beautiful." He paused then, studying me, and I put up a self-conscious hand to make sure my hair still lay in more or less neat ringlets against the fur collar of my gown. "As I told you earlier, you are very lovely, perhaps the loveliest bride to ever come to Harrow Hall. Nevertheless, I think when the spring melt comes, I must take you to Tarenmar so you might get some proper gowns made. It will not do to have the lady of Harrow Hall wearing a wardrobe that is more than thirty years out of date."

Truly, I had thought my borrowed dresses very lovely indeed. Even so, I could not help but experience a stir of excitement at the idea of having an entirely new wardrobe made expressly for me. But it would be so extravagant…. "Do you really think that is necessary?" I asked, hoping I sounded sober and practical and not at all eager. I certainly did not wish him to think that I had married him because of his wealth.

He shook his head at me, laughter kindling in his dark eyes. "Do not be so modest, Bettany. You deserve to have new gowns of your own. Besides, as lord of Harrow Hall, I have a reputation to uphold. While in the past I have had my reasons to stay home, I think I shall visit Tarenmar this spring to pay my respects to the Mark. It would not do to appear there with a new bride who was not properly outfitted for the occasion."

"Oh, well, I would not wish to embarrass you—"

"You will not embarrass me," he broke in. "No woman who looks as you do could be seen as an embarrassment."

Once again I flushed. Dipping my head, I lifted another forkful of venison to my mouth. I had no idea how to respond to his compliments. Perhaps with time I would become used to them, but now....

Linsi whined, almost imperceptibly, and I took a small piece of meat from my plate and lowered it to her. The slightest grazing of her teeth against my fingers, and the meat was gone. Neither of these actions went unnoticed by Doxen, who lifted his head and watched me expectantly.

"I fear you've done it now," Phelan said. "They will not let you alone for the rest of the night."

I looked up at him. "But you told me it would be all right."

"Oh, it will." He grinned. "But I did not say that they would give you any peace once you began feeding them."

Since he was so obviously teasing me, I said loftily, "Then perhaps if you were to offer them some food as well, they would leave me alone."

"I fear it will not be that simple. True, one of them will come to me, but the other will keep guard on you, so that they both might get what they think is their due. Watch." He took a piece of venison between the thumb and forefinger of his right hand, then lowered it next to his chair. At once Doxen got up and padded over to him. The piece of venison disappeared, and the dog sat back on his haunches, gazing up at his master, clearly expecting more.

Meanwhile, Linsi had not moved from her position at my feet. Indeed, since my attention seemed so occupied by her sibling and his master, she gave another of those small whines, as if to remind me that she was still there.

At the sound, Phelan tilted his head in my direction. "You see? We are both well and truly trapped."

"I find that difficult to believe," I retorted. "You are their master, after all, are you not?"

"You have never owned dogs. Is that not what you told me?"

"Yes," I replied, rather gratified he had remembered that small piece of information from our earlier conversation. "But what has that to do with anything?"

"If you had owned a dog, Bettany, then you would know that I am not their master at all. Rather the reverse, in fact."

"Because you spoil them."

He did not appear offended by my comment. Instead, he sat back in his chair, glass of wine in one hand, as he regarded me with some amusement. "Of course I do," he said. "For many years, they have been the only family I had."

The words were spoken simply, but I could hear the echo of loneliness behind them. I at least had my grandmother, but Phelan had only Master Merryk, and there existed no blood ties between them. Was it any wonder that he had bonded so closely with the dogs?

"I understand that," I said, my voice soft. "But now...."

His eyes fastened on mine. For a long moment he didn't stir, only gazed at me. Then he stood and came over to me, his hand outstretched. I took it, and he brought me to my feet. With his other hand, he took a ringlet of my hair and twined it around a finger. "Now," he whispered. "Now we will make a family of our own."

There was no way of misunderstanding his meaning... especially when he bent and claimed my mouth with his, both his hands now tangling in my hair, pulling me close. We had kissed before, but something about this embrace felt different. Perhaps it was the way he drew my body so close to his, everything seeming to touch. I could feel the strength of the muscles pressed against me, feel the heat radiating from his flesh.

The room swam around me. In the next instant, he was gathering me up in his arms, moving away from the dining room and down the suite's short hallway, the one I had guessed terminated in his bedchamber, although of course I had never seen it for myself.

I knew I was about to see it now.

He pushed open the door with one booted foot. Within was warmer than I had expected, for the room had its own hearth with a fire blazing away. I had a confused glimpse of rich red hangings, furniture of dark carved wood, much the same as in the rest of the suite. And the bed—enormous, hung with more deep crimson velvet. A bed where we sank down, Phelan covering my body with his, kisses moving from my mouth down my throat, down the exposed flesh that the wide neckline of the gown revealed.

I thought I had experienced heat before when we kissed, but that was nothing compared to the flush that went through my body then, thrilling me to every extremity. My breaths came in harsh gasps, and I did nothing to stop him when his fingers found the laces at the side of my gown and began pulling at them, loosening the dress so he might begin to slide it up my body.

Some part of my mind wanted to protest, but I knew that was foolish. Phelan was my husband. This was what husbands and wives were expected to do. At any rate, far more of me was eager for his touch, glad when he lifted the heavy gown over my head and tossed it to one side, where it landed on a chair. Then I was clad only in my thin chemise, and yet I was not cold. How could I be, with Phelan there to warm me?

Still, he paused, then said, voice thick with passion, "Get under the covers, beloved."

I would not argue. After pulling back the heavy velvet coverlet and the blankets and sheets beneath, I slipped beneath all the layers, glad enough of their weight despite the fire in my veins. As soon as I had covered myself, Phelan reached up and removed the heavy silver chain from around his neck, and carelessly flung it onto the same chair that barely contained my discarded gown. His doublet soon followed.

My eyes widened at the broad shoulders he'd revealed, the heavy muscles of his arms and chest. Yes, I had seen men without their shirts before, when they worked away in the heat of summer, but none of the men of Kerolton had ever looked the way Phelan did in that moment.

As I stared, he came to the bed and slid under the covers, then pulled me against him. His flesh felt shockingly warm, and I was glad of the way he held me, glad of his warm fingers gliding over me, touching me in places I had never been touched before.

Perhaps I moaned. In that moment, I could not think of anything save Phelan, the heat of his flesh, the waves of pleasure moving through me. And then our bodies were locked together, even as his mouth took mine, stealing my breath as we sank into darkness, two made one, the world disappearing with his touch.

And so it was done.

Chapter Thirteen

Somewhere in the fogginess of my sleep, I had fancied that Phelan's and my joining had changed everything, that when I awoke the next morning, I would see bright sunlight streaming in through the windows, the storm gone and the skies overhead blue once more. But when I opened my eyes, I saw only pale grey light streaming in through the one window where the curtains had been pushed aside.

Phelan stood there, wearing a dressing robe of nearly the same bloody hue as the draperies themselves. It was open down the front, revealing something of the bare, muscled chest I had so admired the night before. He must have heard me stir, for he turned at once as I pushed myself up to a sitting position. My body felt pleasantly sore, and I blushed a little as I thought of the intimacies we had shared just a few hours earlier.

Still, I tried to sound unruffled as I said, "It seems the storm is still with us."

With a smile, he stepped away from the window and came to sit on the edge of the bed. It creaked with his weight, and another flush warmed my cheeks as I thought of the way we had made it creak quite a bit last night. "Yes, the snow still falls," he replied. His hand sought mine where it rested on top of the covers. Even though he had been standing close to the window, and must have felt its drafts, his fingers were very warm as they twined through mine. "But I cannot be too disappointed in that, not when it means I shall be confined to this castle with you."

I supposed he did have a point. There were far worse fates, after all.

"And," he went on, giving my fingers a squeeze, "I told Master Merryk not to disturb us today, so...." The words trailed off significantly, and Phelan arched an eyebrow at me.

Ah, yes, that would be a delightful way to pass a snowy day. Still, I thought I should give my new husband just a little trouble for his presumption. "Not at all? Not even to bring us our breakfast, or dinner?"

"He will knock at the door, then leave a tray outside."

I thought that was a very good way to have a series of cold meals, even if the tray in question was covered. But I did not bother to protest. I would eat cold meals for a month if it meant I could spend so many undisturbed hours with Phelan.

He must have seen the approval in my eyes, for in the next moment he was pushing me down against the pillows, his body on mine again, as once more we sought to lose ourselves in one another, to push back the cold and the storm with the exquisite heat of our joining. As my body shuddered with pleasure, I could only think that I did not care what happened in the rest of the world, so long as I had him with me.

But eventually we must come back to the world, even a world so confined as that of Harrow House. Phelan and I were allowed our one day of grace, to become used to one another, to the rhythms of our bodies and the small shared glances and touches that seemed so much more significant now that we had truly become husband and wife. Master Merryk managed as much as he could, but sometime during those blissful hours Phelan and I had spent together, the drifting snow had broken through the doors that guarded the entrance to the castle's armory, and the lord of Harrow Hall was needed.

He left me with a swift kiss, saying that he would be back as soon as he could. So I must wait once again, albeit in more luxurious surroundings than I'd had in my borrowed chambers elsewhere in the castle. I had all of Phelan's library at my fingertips rather than a few selected books, and I had Linsi and Doxen to keep me company. It was something of a comfort to sit by the fire, Doxen at my feet, Linsi perched within exact reach of my left hand so I might bend down and scratch her ears in the spot she loved the most.

But while I had company, and enough reading material to keep me amused for the hours Phelan must be away, I found myself far more distracted than I should have been. Perhaps it was only that now I knew what it was like to be with him completely, and so to be separated, if only for a short time, was a torture I would not have been able to imagine even a day earlier.

You must learn to tolerate it, I told myself. *He is the lord and master here, and the true steward of Harrow Hall. It shows his love for this place, that he would go to ensure its safety, rather than telling Master Merryk to take care of the matter for him.*

That all seemed well enough, and yet....

Perhaps my unease stemmed merely from my realization that the castle was not quite as impregnable as it seemed. First there had been the roof collapses in the towers, and now this breached door....

It was only a door. Solid oak, I had no doubt, and probably banded with iron, but still not nearly as strong as the grey granite that made up the castle walls. Harrow Hall had stood for hundreds of years, and there was no reason why it should not stand for hundreds more, even in the face of such a fierce storm as the one we'd been suffering for the past week. Some repairs would be made, and then we would all go on.

Linsi pushed her warm, furry head against my idle fingers, letting me know that I was failing in my duty to keep her ears properly scratched. I went back to my task, allowing the book that had been sitting in my lap to slide to one side. Very little I had read had actually stayed in my mind, so I saw little point in continuing the charade. Better to sit here and watch the fire, and wait for Phelan to return.

Which he did many hours later, the doublet he wore smudged with soot and mud, and he himself sporting a streak of dirt along one cheekbone. I rose as soon as he entered the chamber, asking, "Is all well?"

"As well as can be expected." He gave me a tight smile, one I did not find particularly reassuring. As soon as he entered the room, the dogs had abandoned me and gone straight to him, weaving around his legs, tails wagging. After giving them both a few absentminded head scratches, Phelan went on, "We have sealed the breach, and dug out the snow where it was pressing against the wall in that one area, but with it continuing to fall, it is only a matter of time before we'll find ourselves in precisely the same situation once more."

"What will you do?" I inquired, hoping at the same time that there actually was something he could do. I did not want to admit such a thing, but my husband's strength and resourcefulness seemed outmatched when pitted against the power of this storm.

His shoulders lifted, even as he pushed past the dogs and went to the sideboard placed against one wall. From there he lifted a decanter filled with pale gold liquid and poured a measure into a silver cup that had been sitting next to the decanter. "Some *cherbeg?*" he offered, motioning with the decanter.

I had never had the strong liquor, for we did not possess the means of making it back in Kerolton. But the heavy fumes reached me and tickled my nose, making me wish to sneeze. Somehow I managed to refrain, however, then shook my head.

"No, thank you, my husband," I said. "I have been quite warm and comfortable here, and have no need of it. But I am glad you can have some to drive the chill from your bones."

"It is quite effective for that." He raised the cup to his lips and bolted the entire contents in one quick, neat swallow. A small shudder wracked his body, and he gave me a grim smile. "I cannot say I admire the taste overmuch, but it is effective." He set down the empty cup, grimacing slightly as he glanced down at himself. "I am not fit for female company. Let me wash my face and hands, and change. By then supper should be sent up."

Had that many hours passed? I supposed they had. Books and dogs were good company, if not nearly as satisfying as that of my husband. But now he had returned, and we would be able to spend the rest of the evening together.

Until the next crisis raises its head, I thought then. It was not a very charitable notion, so I pushed it aside as best I could, even though I dreaded the prospect of spending more days like one I had just endured, alone with the dogs. Phelan was the lord of this castle, and it was only natural that he should be on hand to manage whatever problems might arise. And now I was the lady of Harrow Hall, and must learn to accept these things as part of my life. Everything about him was new to me now, and so I understood why I would wish to spend every waking moment with him, but that would not always be possible.

He came over and gave me a swift kiss on the cheek, one that felt especially warm against my skin. Perhaps the heat had come from the traces of cherbeg which remained on his lips.

In the next moment he had moved on, going to our bedchamber and the wash basin that sat on a carved oak table in one corner. Sensing he was occupied, Linsi and Doxen settled themselves once more at my feet, all three of us waiting until the lord of the manor bestowed his attention upon us once more.

Well, there were less pleasant occupations, I supposed.

Over the next several days, no more catastrophes were visited upon the castle, despite my worries. Phelan was occupied, true, going with Master Merryk to inspect those sites that might be cause for concern, but despite the ever-falling snow, Harrow Hall seemed to be holding for the moment. And in those hours when I was left alone, I would sometimes lay aside my book or my needlework, and stand at the window and watch the white world outside, and wonder if all of North Eredor had been blanketed in snow, or whether one would only have to ride a few hours southward to escape this endless storm.

I wished that were true. Perhaps I should urge Phelan to go forth with me now, despite the weather, and head south toward Tarenmar. But no, that was a fool's errand, for of course we had no way of knowing how far this covering of snow-laden clouds reached. Still, I found myself craving the sight of the sun and blue skies the way a starving man might long for a solid meal. Even a small glimpse like the one I had had the day Phelan and I first kissed would be better than nothing.

But that glimpse was not given to me. I could take some comfort in my husband's arms at night, when all was safe and warm, and the bleak landscape outside was hidden in blessed darkness. And some nights I did not have even that much, for Phelan seemed to grow increasingly restless, his sleep marred by bad dreams, although when I awoke him to ask what troubled him, he had no answer for me.

"Only nightmares," he said one time, when we held each other in the very early hours of the morning. "I suppose this storm is beginning to prey on my mind as well. Or perhaps," he added with a flashing grin that I could see even in the gloom, "it was that toasted bread with cheese we had instead of a proper dinner. It tasted good at the time, but—"

"It was not the cheese," I said, tone somewhat indignant, since the simple fare had been my idea, something to consume while we sat on the carpet in front of the hearth and soaked up the warmth from the fire that burned therein. "For I had nearly as much as you, and I certainly have had no nightmares."

He shrugged, but I thought I detected something almost studied about the gesture, as if he was in fact more bothered by the dreams than he cared to admit, and wished to hide his concern from me. "Then something else. Bettany, I would be lying to you if I said this storm had not begun to wear on me, and on everyone within this castle's walls. Every day brings a new worry with it."

Some part of me was glad that he had finally decided to admit his concerns, but at the same time, I could feel my heart sink. For if Phelan, who had always seemed so stalwart, had begun to give up hope, what could the rest of us do?

I drew close to him, and he put his arms around me. It was difficult to be overly worried when he held me thus, although I knew the comfort he offered could only extend so far. In here, in this warm and dark chamber, where the glowing coals within the hearth were our sole illumination, it was easy to forget what might be happening elsewhere in the castle, let alone in the outside world.

"It is indeed wearying," I said. "I wish more than anything to venture forth into the sunlight again, to have you kiss me while flowers bloom all around."

"I wish for that as well. And that day will come, Bettany, even though at the moment it seems very far off."

Although the sun was not shining, he did kiss me then, and we progressed to even more pleasurable activities. I was distracted, as I was sure he intended, but I did not forget the restlessness of his sleep, the way his breath had come short and abrupt, his chest rising and falling far too heavily beneath the bulky covers.

How could I forget, when his restlessness seemed to increase with each passing night? It infected me as well, and I found myself unable to find a comfortable position in which to sleep, even though the bed I shared with Phelan was far more luxurious than any I had ever slept in before. At first I wondered if it was merely because he was not used to sharing his bed with another, but I was almost positive that was not the reason. He had slept heavily on our wedding night, and the day after. Ever since then, though, his sleep had grown more and more disordered, and during the days he appeared hollow-eyed and pale. Not so surprising, considering how little rest he was getting, but whenever I attempted to broach the subject, to try to discover why he suddenly was unable to find any solace in sleep, he turned the conversation elsewhere.

It came to me late one afternoon that nearly a week had passed since Phelan and I were married, which meant that I had been residing at Harrow Hall for three full weeks. How such a span of time could have elapsed while a storm still raged on outside, I did not know. We had suffered terrible storms before, of course—I recalled one that blew down out of the north in the winter of my tenth year and lasted for a good five days—but never one that had lasted for well beyond an entire fortnight. And if we were suffering here, in this massive castle of heavy stone, I could only imagine what it must be like in Kerolton.

No, I did not want to imagine such a thing, for that would only awaken my worry for my grandmother, something I had pushed to the back of my mind and attempted to ignore, since there was nothing I could do to help her. I didn't want to think of how our cottage surely must have collapsed under the weight of all this snow, or been buried past its windows. No one could survive in conditions such as that.

I was so lost in these grim visions that I startled when Phelan entered the chamber, then barely contained a gasp of shock. For this—this could not be my husband, this man whose face was white as death, and whose eyes glittered like two pieces of faceted jet. He paused by the hearth, holding his hands out to the fire, and would not look at me.

"My love, what is it?" I exclaimed. "Has the castle suffered another catastrophe?"

"No," he replied. His voice was a harsh rasp, and still he kept his face toward the hearth, so I could see only his profile. "I am—" He broke off then, his hands knotting into fists at his sides. "I am...not well, but it is nothing you need concern yourself with."

"'Nothing I need concern myself with'?" I echoed, disbelief clear in my voice. "I am your wife. If you are ill, then you must let me take care of you."

"No." He pulled in a breath, and even from where I stood I could hear the way it rattled in his breast. "You are my wife, but you are not a healer. Master Merryk will look after me. And," he went on, still with his gaze averted, "I think it best if you would return to the chamber that was yours before we were wed."

This suggestion was so preposterous that I could not prevent myself from moving forward and laying a hand on his arm. "What are you saying, Phelan? What kind of wife would I be, to abandon you when you have need of me?"

A shudder ran through his body, and then he flinched, pulling away from me so I could no longer touch him. "You will be a wife who obeys me! Take your things and go. I would never forgive myself if—if I were to make you ill as well."

None of what he was saying made any sense. If he was truly so ill that he could infect anyone around him, then it was already too late for me. But although his appearance was altered, and he certainly looked as if some fell disease had taken hold of him, I could not quite believe that he was as sick as he wanted me to think. Otherwise, he would not have had the strength to stand there, let alone tear his arm from my grasp with a suddenness that made the tips of my fingers sting as they scraped across the wool of his doublet.

The hateful words, driven by my worry, tumbled from my lips before I could stop them. "Or would you rather say that you are already weary of me, and no longer wish to have me in your presence?"

Perhaps it was only a reflection of the firelight, but I could have sworn I saw that same strange golden flash in his eyes, the one I had detected when we first touched. Voice almost a growl, he snapped, "If that is what you wish to believe, then yes. I cannot think with you underfoot. Go now!"

Never before had I been spoken to in such a manner. I could not believe it was Phelan who addressed me thusly, the man who had praised my beauty, had told me I was the only woman in the world for him. And yet I saw danger in those strangely gleaming eyes of his, and knew I should go if I did not wish to provoke him further. A man who wore an expression such as that might be capable of anything.

So I did what any rational person would do. I fled, without stopping to gather any of my things. As I hurried out the door, I noticed Linsi and Doxen cowering in a corner. Never before had I seen them react to their master's return with anything but outright joy, and the sight of their fear chilled me more than anything else.

But I had come to love those dogs, and I did not wish them to come to any harm. After flicking a quick glance to the door of the bedchamber and noting that Phelan had made no move to pursue me, I called softly to them. "Doxen! Linsi! Come!"

Relief evident in the looks they gave me, they bounded out of the corner where they had been hiding and followed me out to the hallway. I did not quite run, but my pace could not have been considered decorous by anyone who might have observed it. Not that I cared. I only wished to put some distance between my strangely altered husband and myself.

However, I would not hide in the bedchamber that had once been mine. After I had let the dogs in, and petted them and promised them some treats when I returned, I went back out into the corridor. There had to be some reason for Phelan's behavior, something he would not tell me.

So I went in search of the only person who might.

Chapter Fourteen

A group of Phelan's men-at-arms were loitering in front of the fire in the hall. They startled at my entrance, for I had spent most of the time since my marriage to their lord in the upper levels of the castle, and our paths had not had much reason to cross. But at least they did show the proper respect for the lady of the castle, standing up as soon as they spotted me.

"Master Merryk," I said. "Where is he?"

Had I ever sounded so commanding? Truly, I had not been born to a station much given to command. But it seemed something of my urgency communicated itself to the men who stood there before me. One of them stepped forward, and I thought I recognized him. Lewyn, the older man with the grey-flecked hair and bright blue eyes.

Expression not unkind, he asked, "Is something wrong, my lady?"

"N-no," I replied. Of course I would not reveal anything to these men of what had passed between their lord and me. "But I do need to speak with the steward."

"He's in the kitchen, my lady, taking stock of our stores."

At another time, I might have applauded such behavior, for it meant Master Merryk was keeping a careful eye on our supplies. In that moment, however, I could only feel a flash of angry impatience. How dare he be occupied with something so mundane when his master was so terribly altered, so strange?

"Thank you, Lewyn," I said, and I saw a flicker of surprise, followed by gratitude, pass over the man-at-arms' face. Clearly, he had not expected me to recall who he was. "Can you point out the way to me?"

"Through that door"—he gestured with one hand toward a doorway to the left of the great hearth, which roared with flame—"and then on to the end of the hallway. There'll be set of double doors."

I thanked him, then gathered up my skirts and hurried in the direction he had pointed. As I went, I did my best to keep my chin up and my gaze fixed forward. My haste was not all that seemly, but I wanted to appear as in control as possible.

Once I had gone through the doorway Lewyn had indicated and had passed out of sight, I dropped all pretense and ran forward, skirts lifted high above my ankles so I might move more quickly. When I flung open the right-hand door at the end of the hallway and looked inside, I saw a large rectangular room with a cook fire at one end, and long tables lining the walls. Off to one side, a door stood open, revealing a dim space within. From that smaller chamber, which I guessed must be one of the larders, I heard the sound of men's voices—Master Merryk, and someone I did not recognize, who I supposed was probably the cook.

I went in that direction, then paused outside the doorway to the larder. "Master Merryk!"

To my relief, he appeared right away. If he was surprised at my appearing so unexpectedly in the cook's domain, he showed no sign of it. "My lady?"

"I must speak with you," I said. "It is quite urgent."

He did not precisely sigh, but I heard him let out a breath. In that moment, he suddenly looked very tired. "Is it his lordship?"

"Yes," I replied. "He is—he is quite altered, and—"

"Not here," he broke in. "Come, let me take you to my chambers so we might speak."

"But—"

"Please, your ladyship."

What could I say to that? I nodded, and, after calling out a brief farewell to the cook, the steward guided me out of the kitchen and through another short hallway. At the end of that corridor was a single door of scarred oak.

He ushered me inside, to a smallish chamber furnished with simple pieces that would not have been out of place in my grandmother's cottage: a plain square table, equally unadorned chairs. Through a curtained alcove, I spied a narrow bed.

But a fire crackled away in the hearth, and the room was warm enough, especially compared to the chilly corridors outside. Master Merryk pulled out one of the chairs, saying, "Please sit, my lady."

I did as he asked, settling myself on the hard wooden seat. As I did so, he went to a cabinet and pulled out a squat bottle of smoky-colored glass and two small silver cups. He set them down on the table and poured a small measure of pale gold liquid into each cup. The fumes were strong enough to make my eyes water and my nose wrinkle.

"*Cherbeg?*" I asked, surprised that he would offer such a thing to me.

"I think you will have need of it before we are done." He took the chair opposite mine. "His lordship and I had prayed this day would not come, that you would be the cure he sought, but it seems that is not the case."

Ignoring the liquor Master Merryk had set before me, I said, "Cure? So he is ill?"

"It is...a peculiar illness."

My stomach lurched. Could it be that I would lose my husband before I had had the chance to fully know him? I said, voice strained, "Please explain."

For a long moment, the steward did not respond, but took the cup of *cherbeg* and held it before him, not drinking. Perhaps the strength of its fumes was enough to provide something of the effect he desired. When he spoke, his words were measured, heavy. "What I have to speak of to you is a fantastical tale, one you might find difficult to believe. But it is all true. I have witnessed these things, may the gods help me. And I have done what I could to keep my master safe, although you may find that 'safe' is a relative term."

"What is it?" I asked, for the steward's words had already chilled me, even though I had no real idea of what he was trying to explain. "Is it like some brain sicknesses I have heard of, when a person might seem quite well for weeks or even months, and then have a terrible fit of madness?"

"I would that it were so easy to explain." Master Merryk took a healthy swallow of his *cherbeg,* then added, "You would do well to have some of that, my lady, so you may hear what I have to say to you."

Mystified, I raised the cup to my lips and tipped barely a swallow over my tongue. Even that was enough to bring stinging tears to my eyes. I fought back the urge to cough. But then I felt a surge of heat moving down my throat and into my stomach, warming me. For some reason, that heat in the center of my body seemed to give me strength, to give me the will to hear what the steward wished to tell me.

"All right," I said. "Tell me now, Master Merryk. What is it that ails my husband?"

A long pause. Master Merryk looked up from the cup he held and faced me squarely. In his expression, I saw worry... but also a strange kind of resignation, as if he had already confronted the reality of what he was about to say, and had long ago come to terms with it. When he spoke, however, the words were not anything I had expected to hear.

"I suppose, my lady, you have heard of the *corraghar?*"

"Of course," I replied at once, wondering why on earth he had asked me that question. Everyone in North Eredor knew something of the *corraghar,* the wild tribe that lived in the hills to the south and east of the forest of Sarisfell. They had lived separate from us for time out of mind, great hunters and trackers. Indeed, the father of the current Mark had been one of the *corraghar,* although so far it did not seem as if his mixed heritage had done much to bring those wild men into North Eredor's everyday society. I had never seen one of the *corraghar,* however. "They call themselves the people of the wolf, do they not?"

A shadow passed over Master Merryk's face, but he nodded. "Yes, that is what '*corraghar*' means in their tongue."

"So what have they to do with Phelan? His lordship, that is," I amended quickly, thinking the steward might not like me to be quite so familiar with his master's name.

"More than you might think." Master Merryk drained the rest of the *cherbeg* from his cup, then set it down. "As it turned out, his lordship's mother was half *corraghar,* a heritage of which she was entirely unaware. The man who had raised her as his own was not her natural father, and she did not look like one of the hill people at all."

"Do they look so very different from us?" For I had heard nothing about their appearance. It was not a topic that held much importance in Kerolton, since the village was located many leagues from the hills the *corraghar* called their own.

"Their eyes are golden," the steward replied. "Otherwise, they appear much like those of us of the north, save perhaps to be swarthier, and possibly somewhat taller and broader."

Golden eyes. I recalled then those strange flashes of gold within Phelan's own eyes, and guessed they must be something he had inherited from his mother. "I still do not see what the problem is, for our own Mark carries *corraghar* blood within his veins, and it has not seemed to have affected him adversely."

"No, that is true." Master Merryk laid his hands flat on the age-darkened wood of the tabletop, staring at the raised pattern of the veins in his flesh as if he could somehow divine the future therein. "But because of his lordship's...affliction...I made it my mission to learn much more of the *corraghar*. I have lived among them, witnessed their customs, their behaviors."

Affliction? Truly, Phelan had seemed very much afflicted, albeit by something I could not describe. Frowning, I said, "He told me that you would care for him, but if he is truly so ill, should you not be attending to him now?"

The steward offered me a weary smile. "In truth, there is little I can do to help him, except make sure that all the other members of the household are safely out of the way until the... illness...runs its course. I am sure he told you I would look after him so you would not offer to do so. For of course he would never risk hurting you."

"Hurting me? What vile affliction is this, that it would lead to him causing me harm?" I demanded, no longer caring for courtesy, or whether I should allow Master Merryk to speak his piece in his own time.

"'Vile affliction' is a very good way to describe it." He paused, clearly contemplating his next words. "As I said, I lived among the *corraghar* for a time, since I had my suspicions that his lordship's condition was directly related to the strain of *corraghar* blood he carried within him. And so it was that I learned that among the *corraghar* are those they call the *corraghel,* or brothers of the wolf."

"And what has that to do with Phelan?"

"Everything, I fear." The steward ran a finger around the lip of his cup, as if to catch any stray moisture which might remain there. "Tell me, my lady, how much of an open mind do you possess?"

What a question! If it had been posed to me even a few weeks earlier, I might have replied that my mind was as open as that of the next person. Now, though, after spending time in this castle of secrets, of hearing hints about strange powers and dark forces that should have died out long ago, I was beginning to realize that the world contained many things which had never been part of my experience. "Open enough," I said frankly. "Tell me the truth, Master Merryk, no matter how strange it might sound."

He gave me a nod, one that appeared almost approving. "Thank you, my lady. Then I will tell you that the *corraghel* are shape-changers, men who can take on the aspect of a wolf and run with the packs as they would with their own brothers. Hence the name."

"They—they become wolves?" Despite assuring the steward that I wished to hear the truth, no matter how odd it might be, I could not keep the incredulity from my tone. I had never heard of such madness. It must be impossible. And yet....

"Yes. It is nothing to them, a power they can control at will. It is a gift passed from generation to generation. But...." The steward hesitated then, his brows drawing together. "The problem is when a *corraghel* has a child with a woman who is not of the *corraghar*. If that child is female, then there is still no problem, for a woman cannot be *corraghel*. But if that child is a son...."

"Even when he has only a fourth that blood?" I asked, my voice faint.

"Even then, I fear. If that happens, then he cannot control the change. And that is what has happened to Phelan."

"He becomes a wolf." The words came out flat, because in that moment I was not sure what to believe.

"Yes. Each month when Taleron, the larger moon, is full."

"Why a full moon? And why that one, and not small Callendir?"

"I am not sure. I know the *corraghar* perform their rituals to honor the spirits of their ancestors when Taleron is full. So perhaps that tradition also carries on in their blood."

I was silent then, pondering what Master Merryk had just told me. "And there is no way of controlling the transformation?"

"Not really. It is...worse...when there are women about. The change can come on his lordship several days before the moon is full, if he senses their blood."

My cheeks heated at that revelation, but I merely nodded. My moon-blood had come and gone a week before this blizzard descended, and so I had not experienced my courses while residing within the confines of Harrow Hall. "So that is why you have no female servants here."

"Yes. It was easier that way. We could have had older women, those who no longer have their monthly courses, but in the end, we decided it was simpler to not have any women at all."

I supposed I could see the logic of that, so I did not bother to question the situation further. Instead, I ventured, "Then I came here. I suppose he is experiencing the change early, because of my presence."

"No, that is the odd thing." Master Merryk's dark eyes fastened on me, as if he was attempting to probe the very depths of my soul. "The full moon will be tonight, even though we shall not be able to see it, thanks to this unending storm. The change is coming on Lord Phelan at the appointed time, despite you being here. There is something very different about you."

"Is that why he thought I would be the one to break the curse?" I asked, then realized how foolish it was of me to say such a thing. Those words had been spoken in a private conversation, one I should never have overheard.

The steward clearly realized the same thing, for his eyes narrowed, and his mouth compressed before he said, "So you heard that? I will admit that I thought I detected some odd sounds from the corridor while his lordship and I were holding that conversation. Those sounds were you eavesdropping."

"I—I did not mean to," I said quickly. "I had thought I would surprise Phelan by coming to see him, and then I heard the two of you speaking. What you said so engaged my curiosity that I could not find it in me to walk away, even though I knew it was wrong."

"Well, then." Master Merryk tapped his fingers on the tabletop, clearly debating what he should say next. Then I saw his shoulders lift, as if to indicate that we had already gone too far for him to worry about any further revelations. "I fear I have not told you the whole of it. Despite sending the female servants away, his lordship was not entirely safe. He had been betrothed from a very young age to one of the daughters of Lord Olivax, of Blackmore Keep. There was no way to break the engagement without raising Lord Olivax's ire, as well as arousing far too much suspicion. Besides, his lordship believed that as long as he isolated himself from his new bride at the appointed time, then no harm would come to her."

A sick feeling began to grow in the pit of my stomach. Perhaps it was only the *cherbeg* asserting itself, but I feared the anxious roiling in my belly had very little to do with the liquor I had drunk. Certainly there was no sign anywhere in Harrow Hall of the young woman who had been Phelan's affianced bride, not even a portrait in the gallery.

"What happened?" I whispered.

The steward did not look away from me, as some men might have. Voice steady, he said, "She came to us with her servants accompanying her. The wedding was not to take place for several days, as her father had unexpected business arise that required his presence on his own lands. But because he did not wish to violate any of the strictures of the betrothal, he sent his daughter ahead. Pretty girl." A shake of the head before Master Merryk went on, "She was quite enamored of his lordship, and although of course I was not there to see all that passed between them, it was not difficult to guess what happened. Lord Greymount thought he was safe because the full moon was still several weeks off, and Lady Sharenne had no idea of the danger she was in. So they...shared some kind of intimacy...and his lordship changed."

"He—" I had to stop myself there. I could imagine well enough what might have happened next, and I did not want to think of it, did not want to believe that Phelan was capable of such a thing. But could he even be said to be Phelan Greymount, lord of Harrow Hall, when that dreadful change came upon him?

"Yes," Master Merryk said grimly. "I will not go into any detail as to what precisely occurred, my lady, for that is not something you need to hear. We sent word to her father that there had been a dreadful accident, that the Lady Sharenne had fallen down the stairs and broken her neck. Because she had been his lordship's betrothed, with their marriage due to occur within only a few days, no one thought it terribly strange that we buried her here in the family graveyard. It was high summer, a time when a hasty burial would be necessary. Her family was upset, as you might imagine, but his lordship returned her dowry, which did a good deal to mollify her father."

"He did not care that his daughter was dead?" I demanded, unaccountably angered by the steward's description of Lord Olivax's behavior.

"Most likely he was glad to have the dowry returned to him. Lady Sharenne was one of six daughters, and her father had a most difficult time getting them all suitable matches."

I decided it was best to leave that particular matter aside. "So that was why his lordship was so startled that he did not... react...to me."

"Precisely. And that is why he decided you must be the one who could rid him of this terrible curse. Whatever it was that made you different, it was something to keep hold of."

"And so he made me his wife."

"Yes."

Although I had overheard Phelan saying how he thought me beautiful, that he desired me, I still could not help harboring the suspicion that he had married me because he thought I was his only hope of salvation, and not because he truly loved me.

"You doubt," the steward said. "That is understandable, but it is not the truth. His lordship does care for you a great deal, which is why he was cast into despair when the full moon began to approach and he began to feel its effects, despite your presence. He could not understand why he could be with you as a man is with a woman, and yet still have the wolf-change come upon him."

I could not understand it, either, but then again, there was a great deal about this situation that I did not understand. It seemed as if there was some piece of the puzzle still missing, something I should have guessed at by now.

The conversation I had overheard tumbled through my mind, and I began to pick at it, trying to discover something I had overlooked. They had spoken of my birth, and the mystery of my father....

My father. Of course. I knew nothing of him, except it must have been from him that I got my soot-colored locks, so much darker than my mother's. Eyes dark, too, which seemed amiss if he had been one of the *corraghar*, but perhaps the eye color did not always breed true.

"Phelan said my father must have been one of *them*," I said. "Meaning one of the *corraghel*, I take it?"

"That was his suspicion, my lady. And his hope."

"But I have never turned into a wolf."

"Because you are a woman. It is only the men who have that ability."

"Which they can utilize at will."

"Yes, my lady."

My thoughts raced after one another, tumbling. I knew nothing of this father of mine, or why he had lain with my mother, save that she was a great beauty, and perhaps even a man of the *corraghel* had not been able to resist her charms. Putting the mystery of their relationship aside, I thought it seemed clear enough that the corraghel were not tormented by their shape-shifter natures. Why?

Because they have their women to help them stay in control. The thought which surfaced in my mind was so clear-cut that I did not bother to deny it. It made perfect sense. I had been unaware of the blood I carried within me. Phelan had sensed it—hence the spark that had flared between us—but neither of us had had any idea of what to do with it.

But now I did.

Abruptly, I rose to my feet, even as Master Merryk stared up at me in surprise. "When Phelan turns, where does he go?" I asked.

The puzzlement on the steward's features gave way to alarm as he began to divine what I might have in mind. "Out on the moors. I have heard him howling more times than I wish to recall. But you cannot possibly be thinking of going out there—"

"I must," I broke in. "I have to reach out to him now, to show him that I understand what I have to do."

"My lady, he will kill you!"

Those words, spoken so baldly, hung in the air between us. I supposed there was that possibility, that I truly had no idea what I was doing, and so was blindly rushing into danger. But I had to try.

"I would rather die than live without him."

A long silence, and then Master Merryk pushed himself up from his seat. Voice heavy with a mixture of resignation and dread, he said, "Then let me show you."

Chapter Fifteen

I had not wished to waste the time it would require to fetch my mantle from my chamber, and so Master Merryk lent me one of his, along with a heavy knitted scarf and a pair of fur-lined leather gloves that were much too big. My borrowed cloak was likewise too large, and dragged along the ground, but it was warm, and that was good enough for me.

Now we stood at a small door which opened directly from the outer wall. I thought it might lead to the midden where all the castle's waste was dumped, for even in the bitter cold I thought I could smell faint traces of decay, and the way had been carefully shoveled, unlike most of the other entrances to the building. No matter. It was the quickest way outside, and one that would not be noted by any other of the castle's denizens.

Even now, the steward attempted to dissuade me from following what he obviously thought was a mad course of action. "My lady, I beg you—do not do this. We can wait out the moon, and after tonight, his lordship will be himself again."

"Until the next full moon," I said. My voice shook despite my efforts to control it. I had seen what the wolves did to our poor goat Sissi, so I knew exactly what my fate would be if I could not somehow persuade my husband to come back to himself. But I also knew we could not have any sort of life with his terrible half-wolf existence always hanging over us. "Do you not see, Master Merryk? I must try to end this, or nothing will ever change."

His shoulders slumped, and I could see defeat clearly in the lines of his face. In one hand he held a lantern, which he extended to me. I took it from him, seeing in that small gesture capitulation.

Then his chin went up, and he said, "If you overheard my conversation with his lordship, then you also heard me call you a peasant. Now I know that is not a true. You are a very great lady, Bettany Greymount, with a far nobler spirit than many who were born to a title."

Those words moved me greatly, for I knew Master Merryk would not have said such a thing if he did not truly believe it. "I thank you for that, Master Merryk. And I thank you also for your service to his lordship, for I do not believe his own father could have looked after him as well as you have."

Even in the dim light of the lantern, I could see a flush spread on the steward's high cheekbones. He opened his mouth to speak, but in that same moment, a wolf's howl came to us from over the snow-driven moors, chilling me to my bones. I could not entirely blame the icy wind for the cold coursing through me.

"I must go," I said. "Thank you again, Master Merryk."

"May the gods go with you, Lady Greymount."

I could hope for nothing more than that. Turning, I held the oversized cloak shut with one hand, while the one that held the lantern peeked out just enough to illuminate the ground a few feet in every direction. Not that there was so very much to see, for any landmarks had been completely buried after so many days of driving snow. It still fell now, stinging against my face, but I could not allow that to deter me.

A howl sounded once again, this time from somewhere to my left. I set off in that direction, the lantern showing just enough of the ground to keep me from stumbling. Once again I was glad of my sturdy boots. Even so, the cold had already begun to seep up through the soles of my feet.

In that moment, I could not help but wonder what would kill me first, the wolf, or the unending cold.

Neither, I told myself fiercely. *You will find Phelan, and you will call on the* corraghar blood *within you to calm his wolfish soul.*

I could only hope it would be that simple. For of course I had no clear idea of what I was doing, had driven myself out here on the power of a hunch and not much else.

Was it my imagination, or was the snow falling less thickly? Difficult to say, for I held the lantern rather low, thinking it was better that I see where I was walking, rather than worry about what the skies above me were doing.

A few flakes drifted down, and then all went still. Even the icy wind, which had done a very good job of slipping past the heavy scarf wound at my throat, dropped to a whisper and then nothing at all.

Overhead, the clouds parted, and a huge white moon drifted into the blackness the clouds had left behind. The pure silvery light poured down, glittering against the snow. In awe, I looked up, drinking in the moonlight. In that moment, I almost forgot why I had come here.

But I did not forget for very long. From somewhere behind me came a low, harsh growl, and I whirled, barely needing the lantern to see the baleful golden eyes glaring up at me, the smoky darkness of the creature's pelt against the snow-covered ground.

No, not a creature. Phelan.

"My love," I said. My voice shook, and the wolf growled again. Very slowly, I stooped down so I could set the lantern on the ground. Then I spread my hands. "I know you can hear me, Phelan. Come back to me. You need not allow this thing to control you. Let me help you."

The wolf snarled, lip curling to reveal a set of very sharp, very white teeth. I swallowed.

And then, before I could even take another breath, he sprang. Without thinking, I raised my arms, blocking him so he could not reach my throat. But the weight of him knocked me sprawling onto the snow, my head hitting the ground with a hard *thump*. Flashes of red swirled before my eyes, and I blinked. I could not faint now, for then he would surely kill me.

His furry snout was mere inches away from my face. A drop of saliva hit my cheek, but I could not reach up to wipe it away. This was too horribly like my dream, when the wolves set upon me and savaged my throat. I feared, however, that no one would wake me to allow me to escape from this nightmare.

"Phelan, please," I whispered. "I know you are in there somewhere, listening to me. This is not you. It is part of you, just as it is part of me, but it is not *all* of you."

The wolf went very still. His weight on me was growing increasingly painful, but I knew I dared not shift even a fraction of an inch. The golden eyes bored into mine, and yet, I thought I saw a flicker of something there, something which was not a wolf.

Or was I only trying to fool myself into believing there might still be some hope for him?

"This is why we were meant to be with one another," I went on, ignoring the icy dampness of the cloak on which I lay, the bruising weight of the wild animal that held me pinned to the ground. "You recognized that wildness in me, knew it was the one thing you needed, even if you did not know precisely why. I am not telling you to deny the wolf, for it is beautiful in its own way. But you must be its master, just as you are Linsi and Doxen's master. Do you see?"

The wolf growled again. I could smell the stink of its breath, see the bloodshot rims around the golden eyes. There was nothing of my husband in those eyes. This had all been a fool's errand. He would kill me, just as the wolf had killed me in my dream. And I would be buried in the snow, and no one would ever know where my body lay.

Because I did not know what else to do, I breathed out a single word, just as I had in my dream.

"*Please....*"

A long, long moment passed. I dared not look away from the wolf's golden eyes, even though it hurt not to blink, hurt to keep staring up at him. And then I watched as that gold began to dim, turned dark, even as the darkness of his fur grew pale, seemed to alter and lengthen, and became the body of the man I loved.

Phelan Greymount lay there naked in the snow. I let out a sound that was half laugh, half sob, and pulled him to me before pushing us both up from the snowy ground. He looked at me in confusion, his teeth already beginning to chatter.

"What—" he began, and I shook my head.

"You are yourself again, my love. But we must get you back inside." I unbuttoned the cloak I wore and began to pull it from my shoulders.

"No, Bettany, you cannot—"

"I am fully clothed, and have on stout boots and a scarf. We are not so far from the castle that I should suffer much harm by doing without for a few minutes. Please, my love. Take it."

A pause, and then he reluctantly slung the cloak around his shoulders, even as I bent and lifted the lantern. He looked from me to the bright orb of the moon overhead, his features a study in wonder and confusion. "But—"

"It no longer has any power over you, Phelan. But please come."

His eyes were filled with questions, but it seemed he had come back to himself enough to understand that we must get inside as quickly as possible. The going was slightly easier now that the snow no longer fell. Even so, I feared that his feet would be badly frostbitten by the time we reached shelter. I could do nothing about that, however, except hurry him along, glad of the moon lighting our way. Only a few minutes passed before I could see the bulk of Harrow Hall rising before us, the warm candlelight in its windows serving as beacons to guide us home.

And then there was the small door in the outer wall opening, a rectangle of golden warmth that spurred us to hurry those last few yards. Master Merryk waited for us there, shock clear on his features.

But he was not so shocked that he had not prepared for our return, even if he hadn't believed I would succeed. He guided Phelan down the corridor that led to his own rooms, where the fire burned hotter than ever, and a basin of warm water was waiting to bring the life back to his master's poor battered feet.

"Drink this, my lord," Master Merryk said, handing Phelan a cup of *cherbeg*. Yes, that should be just the thing. Its fire would bring some much-needed heat to my husband's chilled body.

With a shaking hand, Phelan took the cup from his steward, then downed its contents. "More," he said, his voice barely above a whisper.

Master Merryk fetched more, and again my husband drank. I looked on anxiously, worried that I might not have gotten Phelan into the shelter of the castle before he suffered permanent damage.

But then he handed his steward the empty cup and glanced over at me. I could see no spark of gold in his eyes, although his gaze was warm enough as his eyes met mine. Improbably, his mouth lifted in a smile.

"The storm is over, is it not?" he asked.

"Yes," I said, relief flooding through me. "Yes, I believe it is."

Truly, the snow had gone. We woke to blue skies and sunshine. I sensed that Phelan had not yet recovered enough to be with me as a husband might be with his wife, but it was enough to hold one another, for me to feel the amazing human beauty of his body pressed against mine. And it was joy uncounted to have him whisper, his face buried in my hair, "You have saved me, Bettany. You have brought me back to myself, and so to you."

Perhaps I could be forgiven for weeping after he told me that.

But although the storm had finally dissipated, there was still much work to be done. Phelan set his men to shoveling out the courtyard, and clearing the area directly in front of the castle's main gates.

"Not that I expect anyone to come visiting any time soon," he commented as we stood in one of the upstairs galleries and watched the men-at-arms throwing great shovelfuls of snow to either side. "But we should at least make the attempt to have it seem as if all is normal here."

"I will need to go visit my grandmother as soon as I can," I said. Yes, I was beyond happy that my husband had been restored to me, and yet I had left connections and responsibilities behind me in Kerolton. I could not neglect them now simply because Phelan's condition was no longer a concern.

"Of course, my love," he replied. "I know that. And as soon as I deem it safe, we will both go. I would like to meet this grandmother of yours so I might thank her for raising such a redoubtable granddaughter."

"Oh, so I am redoubtable, am I?" I returned, looping my arm through his.

"You know you are, my remarkable, wonderful Bettany. You refused to give up, even though I had long ago."

"I would say that was more me being stubborn," I said, then went up on my tiptoes so I might kiss him on the cheek. "Or perhaps ignorant. You had been fighting against your fate for many years, whereas it was all very new to me. I did not know better."

"Then thank the gods for your ignorance, if that is what you wish to call it. Because without you—"

He broke off there, dark eyes haunted, and I immediately put my arms around his waist so I could hold him close. "But the gods did send me to you, Phelan," I said. "I will admit that I have not had much use for them prior to this, but I can think of no other reason why I would have come here."

A corner of his mouth lifted, and I was glad to see some portion of his usual insouciance return to his manner. "I thought you came here to beg me to pay your taxes."

"To allow me extra time to pay my taxes," I said, my tone mock-severe. "I most certainly did not ask you to pay them for me."

"Ah, I suppose that is the truth of it. I know you have a difficult time asking for anything from anyone. A handout is certainly not something you would willingly ask for."

"I would think not," I replied with some indignation. "I would never have expected such a thing."

"Of course you would not," Phelan said with a smile. "But I will pay those taxes, since you are now my wife, and it is my duty. And my pleasure," he added, then bent down and kissed me.

I had not even thought of that. But because he was my husband, my obligations were now his as well.

I could only hope they would all be so easy to discharge.

It was nearly a ten-day after the Great Storm—as everyone had taken to calling it—had passed before both Master Merryk and my husband agreed that the weather seemed calm and clear enough to risk the journey to Kerolton. During that time, my moon-courses had come and gone, telling me I was not yet with child...and also reassuring both Phelan and myself that he could be around me while I was in such a state and not succumb to his wolf nature. This greatly reassured the two of us. As for the other matter, well, I wished very much to have his child, but I did not mind waiting just a little while. It was good for the two of us to know one another as husband and wife before we also must be acquainted with each other as parents.

We set out for Kerolton on a fine day, with the sun shining down upon us and a pleasant wind at our backs. The weather had been nowhere near warm enough to even begin to melt the massive snow drifts that had piled up during the Great Storm, but the going was easier than I had feared, the sturdy horses we rode making their way across the wintry landscape without flagging.

When the trees of the Sarisfell woods appeared in the distance, I felt my heart lift, for I knew we did not have that much farther to go. We had already decided to go to my grandmother's cottage first. If she had abandoned it during the storm, by this time she would most likely have returned, as long as the place was still habitable. And if not, then we would head off to look for her in the village.

I would not let my mind go any further than that. I had to believe she was safe, that she had taken refuge in Kerolton before the storm grew too fierce.

Our party was small enough: Phelan and myself and four of his men-at-arms. Master Merryk had remained behind to keep watch on Harrow Hall—as well as to make sure the repairs on the castle would continue in a timely manner. Once we had entered the forest, I took the lead, as I was the only one who knew the location of our destination.

But when we entered the clearing where my grandmother's cottage stood, I found myself pulling the horse I rode to an abrupt stop. For the cottage was a ruin of broken plaster and splintered timbers, the only thing still standing the chimney, and even that had become a sad stub, half its bricks tumbled into a pile in the snow.

Although I had feared something like this, seeing the reality of it was enough to bring a strangled sob to my throat. Phelan spurred his horse forward and came up beside me. "My love," he said, "I am sure your grandmother is safe. You yourself told me that most likely she would have sheltered in the village once she saw how bad the storm had become."

I could but nod, as I did not trust myself to speak. In that moment, I was glad of the presence of the men-at-arms, for if I had been alone with Phelan, I had no doubt I would have burst into tears.

After swallowing past the thickness in my throat, I said, "You are right, my husband. We will go there now, and no doubt we will find her teaching Master Willar's daughters how to spin properly, for I know that his wife is none too gifted at the task."

"I am sure of that, dear wife," Phelan said. "You may continue to lead, as you know the way better than the rest of us."

I blinked back the remnants of my tears, then nodded as I turned my horse around. Once again we made our way through the winter woods, although the sun was not quite as fine and bright in here among the thickets of pine and fir. But the paths were clear enough, seeming to indicate that people had been coming and going in this area, probably to gather firewood and to hunt what squirrels and rabbits they could find.

After a few more minutes, we came out of the woods and into the open fields that surrounded the village. Here, the snow looked more or less untouched, except for paths that appeared to have been laboriously carved through the heavy snow. I also spotted the tracks of deer and other woodland creatures, showing that not all had perished in the Great Storm.

And then I saw smoke rising from the chimneys of the village houses, pale against the hard blue sky. As we approached, I was relieved to note that the buildings here appeared to have fared better than my grandmother's cottage. Yes, snow was piled up in enormous drifts everywhere I looked, but the doorways were clear. Many of the houses had their windows boarded up, a necessary precaution against the weight of the accumulating snow. But the smoke told me that people had survived. There was life here.

I guided my horse toward Amery Willar's home, thinking it was with him I would receive the most favorable reception, even if my grandmother had ended up sheltering elsewhere. We came to a stop in front of his house, where a narrow path had been carved out between the drifts blocking his boarded-up windows.

Phelan dismounted first, then came to me so he could help me down from the saddle. I had been given a docile horse to ride and so had fared well enough on the journey here, but I was still awkward on horseback, as of course my grandmother and I had been too poor to own a horse or even a pony, and so I had never learned to ride with any degree of skill.

The feel of my husband's strong, gloved fingers reassured me somewhat, and I settled my cloak on my shoulders and smoothed the front of my gown before stepping forward so I might knock on the door. A long pause followed that knock. I cast a nervous glance at Phelan, but he only smiled, head cocked to one side, as if amused by my impatience.

Then the door opened, and Amery Willar stared out at me, blue eyes widening so much that I feared they might pop out of his head. "B-Bettany?"

"Yes, Master Willar. I am glad to see that you appear to have weathered the storm well enough. May we come in?"

At the word "we," Amery's gaze shifted past me to Phelan. The richness of my husband's dress, and the band of silver that held his heavy dark hair back from his brow, made his identity clear enough. If possible, Master Willar's eyes widened even further. "M-my lord?"

"Yes, Master Willar," Phelan said. "I am Lord Greymount. Mistress Sendris took refuge in my keep during the storm, and now she has some news for her grandmother. Is she here?"

"Why, yes, she is, my lord," Amery replied, and a great rush of relief went over me. Ever since I had seen the ruin of the cottage, I had feared the worst, but it seemed I would not have to mourn her after all. "My youngest brought her here when the snow began to fall so thickly, and she has sheltered with us the entire time." He paused, then waved a hand, ushering us inside. "But here I am talking while you stand out in the cold. Please come in, my lord."

Phelan offered him a pleasant smile, then took my hand and brought me into the house. I had been there once or twice; we now stood in the small entry hall, and two short corridors led off in opposite directions, one toward the wing where the bedrooms were located, and the other toward the more pub-lic areas of the house—the sitting room and dining room and kitchen. From that direction I heard the sound of voices, and it was there that Amery led us, looking back over his shoulder from time to time, as if he could not quite believe the evidence of his own eyes.

Although they had not been invited in, the men-at-arms came inside as well, although they waited in the entryway rather than accompanying us to the sitting room. Just as well, for the place would have been quite crowded if they had attempted to squeeze in there with us and the rest of Amery's family.

The sitting room was good-sized chamber, with a large fireplace on one wall and a floor of smoothly sanded oak. Gathered around the hearth was a group of women—Amery's wife and daughters. Sitting in the center of all of them was a woman with sleek, grey-streaked hair, a woman who turned along with all the rest of them to see who had just entered the room.

Her hand went to her mouth. She had been holding a drop spindle and a fluffy bunch of carded wool, but they both fell to the floor as she caught sight of me. Her face was pale. Indeed, she had the appearance of someone who had just seen a ghost. Not so strange, I supposed, for she must have surely thought me dead, perished weeks ago in the howling blizzard that had swept down upon us all.

I let go of Phelan's hand and moved forward, my skirts of fine wool whispering over the wooden floor. Standing behind my grandmother was Amery's daughter Vianna; her eyes narrowed as she cast an envious glance at the rich clothing I wore. Yes, it was quite out of date, but still finer than anything she owned.

"I am so glad you were able to take refuge here," I said to my grandmother, doing my best to ignore the stares from the female members of Amery's family. His two boys must have been out hunting, or perhaps gathering wood for the fire. "Just as I was able to take refuge in Harrow Hall."

My grandmother's gaze flicked toward Phelan and back to me. "So you were able to reach the castle safely."

"Yes," I said. Perhaps later I would tell her how I had nearly perished in the cold before Phelan's men found me, but I saw no reason to go into such detail right then, for I thought that information would only upset her unnecessarily. "I did wait out the storm there, and was given all consideration and kindness. Indeed"—I paused then, and sent a quick glance toward my husband. He inclined his head, encouraging me to continue—"indeed, I was made so welcome that Lord Greymount and I formed quite an attachment. We were married a little more than a fortnight ago."

This declaration elicited a gasp from the members of Amery's family, while the man himself gave me another of those pop-eyed stares. My grandmother went very still, then stood up straighter as she looked past me to the lord of Harrow Hall.

"You love her?" she asked.

Another gasp from the assemblage. Clearly, they did not possess the courage to have asked such a question, and so were shocked to see that my grandmother apparently did.

Quite calmly, Phelan replied, "More than life itself. Indeed, she is my life. I thank the gods daily, for they were the ones who sent her to me."

This answer made my grandmother nod in some approval. Then she glanced back over at me. "And I suppose you love him."

"Of course I do," I said stoutly. "You know me well enough, Grandmother, to know that I am not swayed by wealth."

"Or a title?" she asked.

"Or a title," I responded. "I would have married him even if he had been Kerolton's poorest woodcutter."

"Fortunately for both of us," Phelan put in them, "I am no such thing. I am able to give your granddaughter the comforts and ease that she deserves. The same comforts and ease I am now offering to you. It was very noble of Master Willar to offer you shelter here, but just as Harrow Hall is now her ladyship's home, it shall be your home as well."

"I am no grand lady, to live in a castle," my grandmother said. Bold words, I supposed, but since I knew her so well, I could hear the hesitation beneath them. Yes, it would take some time for her to adjust to the alteration in her situation. I understood that, but we all understood as well that her own home had been destroyed, and she could not stay with the Willar family indefinitely. At any rate, she was my family, and she needed to be with me and Phelan.

"I did not think I was, either," I said. "But I have lately conceded that there is much to be said for such a life. So come with us, Grandmother."

"Would you not wish to be there to watch your great-grandchildren grow up?" Phelan inquired.

My grandmother shot a quick glance at my waistline, although even if I were with child—which I knew I was not—I would not be showing any evidence of such a condition. Then she let out a small breath. "You are a clever one, Lord Greymount, to know exactly how to persuade an old woman. Very well. I will come with you. No doubt the Willars will be glad enough to have me out from underfoot."

This comment provoked a half-hearted protest from Mistress Willar, one which my grandmother pointedly ignored. It could not have been easy to have a houseguest for such an extended period of time under such trying conditions.

"I will gather my things," my grandmother said. "They aren't many, so it shan't take me very long. But I will also have to chase down Malkin," she added, then left the room, clearly headed to the wing of the house that contained the bedchambers.

"Malkin?" Phelan inquired with a lift of the eyebrow.

"Her cat," I explained.

"Ah." His lips quirked. "We shall have to see what Linsi and Doxen make of that."

"As they are very well-behaved dogs, I am sure they will be just fine."

Phelan smiled, even as he shook his head. But, since he seemed to note how the Willar family was staring at the two of us, he filled the awkward silence by saying in that easy manner of his, "Please know, Master Willar, that if there were any costs incurred by housing Mistress Sendris—and Malkin—here for so many days, I would be happy to compensate you for them."

"N-no, of course not," Amery Willar replied at once. A flash of irritation passed over his daughter Vianna's face, while his wife only appeared resigned, as if she had known that her husband would never accept such an offer, even if doing so could only benefit his family.

"You are certain?"

"Very certain," Amery said. "We were honored to shelter Mistress Sendris here."

In that moment, my grandmother returned. In one hand she held a small battered leather satchel, one I knew she had brought with her to the forest of Sarisfell many, many years ago when she came here to be my grandfather's wife. In the other was a large wicker cage, from which emerged a low growl.

Malkin had never much enjoyed being transported in such a manner.

"I will warn you," she said. "I am not a very good horse-woman."

"No matter," Phelan replied. "Neither is your granddaughter, and so we shall set an easy pace."

At that response, she chuckled, and I could feel myself begin to relax. My grandmother was not one for easy laughter, and if you were lucky enough to amuse her, it meant she thought well of you.

"But because of that pace," my husband went on, "we should go now, so we have plenty of daylight to guide us home."

"Sensible of you."

Then she turned and thanked Amery and his wife for their hospitality, added a few words to the girls in praise of their improved spinning—leaving Vianna out of that compliment, I noticed—and headed out to the entryway. Phelan and I followed. His mouth was pursed with amusement, and I guessed that he was rather looking forward to having someone under his roof who was not particularly impressed by him.

But once we were outside, he appeared sober and respectful enough, relieving my grandmother of her burdens and handing them off to our escort, then guiding her into the saddle of the horse we had brought for her before he did the same thing for me. The men-at-arms also mounted, and in no time we were headed out of Kerolton and into the forest.

Phelan and I rode just far enough ahead of our companions that we were able to exchange a few words in relative privacy. "You did not mention what a singular person your grandmother was," my husband remarked.

"I thought it best for you to find out on your own."

His teeth flashed in the sunlight as he grinned. "I suppose I can see the wisdom in that." Then a wicked gleam entered his eyes, and I shot him a look of mock alarm.

"My husband, what is it you are planning?"

"You shall see."

I lifted an eyebrow.

Appearing to relent, he said, "I was just thinking that since I have found wedded bliss, perhaps it is time for Master Merryk to discover those same joys. I think he must be of an age with your grandmother, or perhaps only a few years older."

"And I think you must have taken leave of your senses. They would never suit. It would be the irresistible force and the immovable object!"

"Perhaps." A sly grin touched his mouth. "But it will be highly amusing to watch, don't you think?"

"'Amusing' is one word for it, Phelan Greymount. I would think you would want some peace in your household, after all that you have been through."

The smile faded, and his expression grew deadly serious. "I have never been much of one for peace. Happiness, on the other hand...." The words trailed away, and he sent me a piercing look, one which awoke a familiar heat in the pit of my belly. "You have made me happy, Bettany. Is it foolish to want those around me to be happy as well?"

"Not at all," I replied. "It is wonderful. *You* are wonderful."

He sidled his horse up next to mine, and before I knew precisely what was happening, he had plucked me out of his saddle and deposited me before him. Vaguely I could hear my grandmother gasp, but I paid her reaction little mind. How could I, with Phelan's arms around me and his voice a fierce growl in my ear as he said, "Promise me it will always be like this."

"It will," I said. "Or even better. Always."

He kissed me then, kissed me in the brilliant sunshine with its promise of brighter days. And I did not care who watched, because I understood more than ever that he was the only one who could make my heart sing like this, could make the blood rush in my veins and warm me all over.

Phelan Greymount kissed me, and I was happy.

The End